"You're attending church again?" Bryan's voice was cautious, as if he still couldn't quite believe it.

"Yes."

Bryan was tempted to ask Amy how she'd found her way back to God. But that was too personal. And their relationship was strictly business now.

"Well, I need to get back to work," he said.

"And I need to get home and have some dinner."

Without waiting for a response, Amy left. She was still trembling when she stepped off the elevator. She wanted to attribute her reaction to the shock of being startled in the deserted office, to the fear that an intruder had trespassed onto family property, but she knew better. She trembled now from fear of another kind, sparked by the knowledge that an intruder had, indeed, trespassed tonight. Onto her heart. And that he'd taken something of great value, something she desperately needed for peace of mind. For survival, even.

Gone was the last illusion that Bryan Healy was history.

* * *

DAVIS LANDING:
Nothing is stronger than a family's love

Books by Irene Hannon

Love Inspired

*Home for the Holidays #6
*A Groom of Her Own #16
*A Family To Call
   Her Own #25
It Had To Be You #58
One Special Christmas #77

*Vows
†Sisters & Brides

The Way Home #112
Never Say Goodbye #175
Crossroads #224
†The Best Gift #292
†Gift from the Heart #307
†The Unexpected Gift #319
All Our Tomorrows #357
The Family Man #366

IRENE HANNON

is an award-winning author who has been a writer for as long as she can remember. She "officially" launched her career at the age of ten, when she was one of the winners in a "complete-the-story" contest conducted by a national children's magazine. More recently, Irene won the coveted RITA® Award for her Love Inspired book *Never Say Goodbye*. The RITA® Award, which is given annually by Romance Writers of America, is considered the "Oscar" of romance fiction. Irene, who spent many years in an executive corporate communications position with a Fortune 500 company, now devotes herself full-time to her writing career.

In her spare time, she enjoys performing in community musical theater productions, singing in the church choir, gardening, cooking and spending time with family and friends. She and her husband, Tom—whom she describes as "my own romantic hero"—make their home in Missouri.

IRENE HANNON

THE
FAMILY
MAN

Steeple
Hill®

Published by Steeple Hill Books™

ACKNOWLEDGMENTS:
Special thanks and acknowledgment are given
to Irene Hannon for her contribution
to the Davis Landing miniseries.

To Tom…always.
And to Carolyn…one more time!

STEEPLE HILL BOOKS

Steeple
Hill®

ISBN-13: 978-0-373-81278-3
ISBN-10:   0-373-81278-7

THE FAMILY MAN

Copyright © 2006 by Harlequin Books S.A

I know that You can do all things,
and that no purpose of Yours can be hindered.
—*Job* 42:2

The Hamiltons of Davis Landing

Nora McCarthy – m – Wallace Hamilton

| Jeremy* | Timothy | Amy | Christopher (t) | Heather (t) | Melissa |

*(son of Nora and Paul Anderson)

Legend
m = married
t = twins

Chapter One

"I have a résumé for the freelance position that you might find interesting. The writer seems to have a lot of expertise in family issues, just like you wanted."

Amy Hamilton spared her sister a quick, distracted look, then went back to reviewing the layouts for the next edition of *Nashville Living* magazine. "I don't need to see it. You're the features editor. Just weed through the applicants and find some good people for us to interview."

Heather tucked a soft wave of long brown hair behind her ear, took a deep breath and stood her ground. "I think you should look at this one."

Stifling a sigh, Amy prayed for patience— a virtue she sometimes found in short supply. Always driven, always a high achiever, she hated to waste time. As managing editor of

Hamilton Media's popular lifestyle magazine, she didn't need to be involved in the nitty-gritty of sorting through applications. She trusted Heather to select the best candidates. Maybe more than Heather did, Amy reminded herself. In recent years Amy had come to realize how difficult it had been for Heather to live in the shadow of her successful and popular oldest sister, with the inevitable comparisons—and insecurity—that brought. So more and more she tried to factor that into their relationship, taking extra time to let Heather know that she was appreciated and respected.

"Okay. What have you got?" Amy pushed the layouts aside and gave her sister her full attention.

The rigid line of Heather's shoulders eased, and she entered the office, handing Amy the résumé as she spoke. "It came from a recruiter. I have a feeling the candidate may not even know it was forwarded to us."

Planning to give the résumé only a quick perusal before passing it back to Heather, Amy focused on the section delineating the applicant's experience. Impressive, she noted, as she scanned the credentials. An eight-year stint at a daily paper, most recently doing feature work—much of it family related.

"Sounds promising." Amy held out the résumé to Heather. "I assume you're going to call her for an interview?"

"It's a him."

A flicker of surprise darted across Amy's face. She'd just assumed any writer interested in family topics would be a woman. But that was reverse chauvinism, she chided herself. There was no reason a man with the right qualifications couldn't do this job. She, of all people, should be sensitive to gender stereotypes, considering her ongoing rivalry with her two older brothers, who held the choicest positions in the family business. Still, the magazine job suited her and she harbored no resentment about the distribution of duties. Besides, considering the mess things were in right now at Hamilton Media, she was glad she was out of the line of fire.

"Okay. Him," Amy corrected herself.

Instead of taking the proffered document, Heather gave her an odd look. "Check out the name."

Something in her sister's expression and tone put Amy on alert. Curious, she pulled her arm back and scanned the personal data at the top. It took her only a second to find the name.

Bryan Healey.

The man who had broken her heart.

Several seconds ticked by as Amy stared at the name. As she thought about the earnest, auburn-haired high-school senior who had professed his undying love, and asked her a few months later to be his wife. But much as she'd cared for Bryan, the timing hadn't been right. She'd had too many things she wanted to do before tying herself down with the obligations of marriage and a family. So she'd asked for time—and space—suggesting that they both date other people before making a permanent commitment. Though he'd agreed in the end—with reluctance—they'd begun to drift apart. And after the time he'd shown up unannounced a few months later on her campus, she hadn't heard from him again. Memories of that unexpected visit never failed to bring an embarrassed flush to her cheeks. Still, she'd loved Bryan and been confident that when she was ready, he'd be available. That he'd wait for her. But he hadn't. He'd married someone else. Started a family. Moved away. And left her heart in tatters.

It was one of the few times in Amy's life when things hadn't gone her way, and she could still recall with vivid intensity the shock that had rippled through her the spring of her senior year in college when Heather had given her the news of Bryan's engagement. That initial shock had given way to hurt, then to anger. In the end, she'd written him off, telling herself things were better this way. That he'd been the wrong man for her anyway, and that someday the right one would come along.

Except he never had. At thirty, Amy wasn't exactly over the hill. But unlike her high school and college years, when she'd had more dates than she could handle, her social life now was pretty bleak. Partly because her job kept her too busy...and partly because Bryan had ruined her for anyone else. The simple fact was that in all the years since they'd parted, she'd never found anyone who could measure up to him.

"So what do you want to do?" Heather prompted, when Amy didn't respond.

Prodding her brain into action, Amy leaned back in her chair, her casual posture and tone conveying none of her inner turmoil. "What do you think we should do?"

"He's got all the right qualifications."

She couldn't argue with that. But even though she'd gone on with her life, even though their relationship was ancient history, even though she'd learned to accept the fact that

Bryan wasn't the partner God intended for her, it would still be awkward to have him around. "Don't you have any other strong candidates?"

"None that can match Bryan's experience. Besides, I think he needs the job."

"Why?"

"The recruiter sent a cover note. Bryan's paper in Missouri has been acquired by a syndicate, and they eliminated a lot of the staff writers on August first. So Bryan decided to come home. It can't be easy for him, Amy. Losing his wife, raising his son alone…he's had some tough breaks, from everything I've heard."

Amy knew about his wife's death. She also knew that he had a son. Though the Healeys and the Hamiltons had never traveled in the same social or economic circle, nor shared the same friends, Heather had managed to keep tabs on Bryan. Probably through Betty at the Bake-shoppe, who always had her ear to the ground. Sometimes Amy had wondered if Heather carried a secret torch for Bryan herself. Not anymore, of course. Not since Heather's fiancé, *Nashville Living* staff photographer Ethan Danes, had come along and stolen her heart.

When Amy didn't respond, Heather tilted her head and gave her sister a speculative look. "You don't still have feelings for him, do you?"

"Of course not."

The skeptical expression on her sister's face told Amy that her reply had been too prompt and too vehement. So she decided that offense was the best defense—even if the offense was a weak one. "But I always thought *you* did."

The ploy didn't seem to fool Heather—or ruffle her. "I like Bryan. I always did. Most of your boyfriends treated me like a piece of furniture. Bryan not only noticed me, he always took the time to say a few nice words. He was a genuinely nice guy. But no one compares to Ethan." Her face softened, and a smile whispered at the corners of her lips before she got back to business. "Anyway, I think we ought to consider him. Under normal circumstances, I would have scheduled an interview without even consulting you. But I wasn't sure how you'd feel about this."

Toying with her pen, Amy debated her next move. Heather's comment about Bryan's difficulties tugged at her conscience. She supposed she should at least consider interviewing him. After all, when his recruiter told him where the interview was, he'd probably decline, anyway. *She* would, if the circumstances were reversed. Despite the fact that they'd both moved on with their lives, the history between them would make the situation very awkward. She couldn't imagine why he'd want to put himself through that kind of stress. But at least, by offering an interview, she'd be able to soothe her conscience with the knowledge that she'd given him the opportunity.

With sudden decision, Amy pulled the layouts back toward her. "Go ahead and set up an interview."

"Is later this week okay?"

"Fine."

As Heather left, Amy tried to transfer her attention back to the material in front of her. She'd always been able to switch focus in a heartbeat, to concentrate on the task at hand. For some reason, though, that skill deserted her today. Instead, memories of Bryan kept intruding on her consciousness. And she couldn't still the nervous flutter in her stomach at the thought that he might accept the invitation to be interviewed.

But that was a remote possibility, she reassured herself. In all probability, he would find the thought of renewing their acquaintance just as uncomfortable as she did. She was pretty sure that nothing would come of the recruiter's submission. At least, nothing job related.

The effect on her heart was a different story, though. For almost ten years, she'd refused to let thoughts of Bryan disrupt her life. First, by using anger and a sense of righteous indignation. Then by keeping herself so busy she had little time to dwell on the past. Yet their split had nagged at her, deep in the recesses of her heart. Perhaps that had been one of the reasons she'd found her way back to God a couple of years ago, after a long absence. Only then, after much prayer, had she finally made her peace with the rift, accepting that God had other plans for her. But if that was true, why had the conversation with Heather unsettled her? Why did the possibility that her path might again cross Bryan's rattle her?

Amy didn't have the answer to those questions. Not that it mattered anyway, she told herself. The odds that Bryan would accept the interview were minuscule, at best. In all likelihood, he'd find a job with a Nashville paper. Considering that he had a young son to raise, he had to be looking for a full-time job, not a part-time freelance position. That alone should eliminate the job at *Nashville Living* from consideration.

Consoled, Amy went back to work.

* * *

"Bryan accepted the interview. He's scheduled for Thursday at nine o'clock."

With a startled jerk, Amy turned from her computer screen to stare at Heather, who stood in her office door. "What?"

"Bryan. Nine o'clock Thursday." Heather gave Amy an intent look. "What's wrong?"

Amy tried to erase the shock from her face. "Does he know I'll be involved in the interview?"

"I told the recruiter, and he said he'd pass that along. I assume he did. I have two other candidates, too. One is scheduled for tomorrow morning, one Thursday afternoon. Here are their résumés." Heather walked in and laid them in Amy's in basket. "I knew you'd want to review them before the interviews."

A couple of beats of silence ticked by. "Why don't you handle the interviews alone this time?"

A quizzical expression flitted across Heather's face. "You always sit in on interviews for writers."

Shrugging, Amy turned back to her computer. "This is just a freelance position. I trust you to pick the best person." Although her comment and actions were designed to end the conversation, she sensed that Heather hadn't moved. A quick glance over her shoulder confirmed her suspicion. Her sister was still standing on the other side of her desk, hands on hips, frowning. "What?" Amy demanded.

"I thought you said you didn't still have feelings for Bryan."

"I don't."

"Then how come you don't want to see him?"

"I didn't say I didn't want to see him. I've just got a lot on my plate right now. You can handle this."

"You've never missed an interview before."

Irritated, she glared at Heather. "There's a first time for everything, okay?"

At the snappish tone in her voice, Heather looked hurt—and surprised. "I'm sorry. I didn't mean to upset you."

Taking a deep breath, Amy counted to three. She never lost control. Especially at the office. Even in the most unpleasant circumstances, she made it a point to maintain a professional, even-keeled manner. Sometimes that was difficult in a family business. But she'd never slipped. Until today. "No, I'm the one who's sorry. But I want you to handle this, okay?"

"Yeah. Sure. I have to get back to work."

As Heather turned, her stiff posture told

Amy that she had some fences to mend with
her sister, as well as some explaining to do
about her unprofessional—and uncharacteristic—behavior. And she'd take care of it. Just
as soon as she figured out a way to explain it
to herself.

The reception area at Hamilton Media,
which housed the offices for both *Nashville
Living* and the *Davis Landing Dispatch*—one
of the town's two newspapers—was bright
and cheerful, conveying an upbeat mood.
Colorful paintings adorned the walls, and
large windows allowed the late-summer
sunlight to spill into the space, which retained
much of the historic charm expected from a
building approaching the century mark. Under
other circumstances, Bryan would have found
the setting pleasant and relaxing. But his
nerves were too much on edge to be soothed
by anything today.

Ever since he'd agreed to this interview,
he'd been besieged by doubts. He had no
desire to see Amy Hamilton again. Despite
the fact that any feelings he'd had for her had
died long ago, thoughts of her still left a bitter
taste in his mouth. But he needed a job, and so
far nothing else had come up. A part-time free-

lance slot wasn't ideal, by any means. That meant no insurance, for one thing. And he had to have insurance. Hard experience had taught him the value of that benefit. COBRA from his previous employer was providing interim coverage, but it was expensive. He needed to hook up with a full-time position that would offer health care coverage at a more reasonable cost—and sooner rather than later. But in the meantime, at least this job would provide some much needed cash. Living with his father would help ease his money problems in the short term, but he didn't want to wear out their welcome. Even though his dad seemed to be enjoying the company. And even though Dylan wouldn't mind staying at his grandpa's house forever.

Thoughts of his son brought a smile to his face. It was hard to believe he'd be starting kindergarten in two weeks. Harder still to believe that Darlene had been gone for five and a half years.

Like the sun disappearing behind a storm cloud, Bryan's smile faded. All his hopes of creating a warm and loving family had died with his wife. So had his faith. Once strong, it had crumbled in the face of her tragic death, as he'd watched his son struggle for life, as he'd tried to take on the job of both mother and father. Dylan had been the only bright spot in his life these past few years. Protecting him, providing for him, had become his top priority. And only a priority that vital could have compelled him to go on this interview…and face a past he thought he'd left far behind.

"Mr. Healey? You can go up now."

The querulous voice of Herman Gordon caught Bryan's attention. The stooped, gray-haired gent and his wife, Louise, had been with Hamilton Media since before Bryan had been born. Long retired from their regular positions, they now served as gatekeepers, presiding over the marble-floored lobby with dignity and unquestionable authority. Despite their advanced years and grandparentlike demeanors, nobody, but nobody, got past the Gordons without an appointment. They were an institution in Davis Landing.

"Right this way, young man." Herman led Bryan toward the elevator with a sprightly step that belied his age, then waited while Bryan stepped inside the dark-paneled cube that gleamed with polished brass. "Heather Hamilton will meet you on the second floor."

As Bryan nodded his thanks, the door slid closed. The elevator began to rise…and so did his pulse. In mere minutes he would be face-to-face with Amy—the woman he'd once loved. His grip tightened on the handle of his portfolio, and he tried to take a few deep, calming breaths. But the effort had little effect. The best he could hope for would be to feign a semblance of outward calm despite the sudden churning in his stomach. And it didn't help that he was on unfamiliar turf—*her* turf.

Although Bryan and Amy had dated for more than a year, he'd never been past the lobby of the impressive three-story brick building on Main Street that housed the offices of Hamilton Media. Her father, Wallace, hadn't approved of him, so he'd steered a wide berth around the old man, whose domineering presence had been more than a little intimidating to a nervous teen from the other side of the tracks—or, in this case, from the other side of the river. The physical separation between affluent Davis Landing and blue-collar Hickory Mills might be only as wide as the scenic Cumberland River, but the two sections of town were light-years apart in every other way. Bryan had been keenly aware of that division the few times he'd been in Wallace's presence. The patriarch of the Hamilton Media dynasty had struck

Bryan as invincible, a man who knew what he wanted and didn't let much stand in his way of getting it.

But he hadn't been invincible after all, as recent events had demonstrated. According to Bryan's father, Wallace had been seriously ill with leukemia for some time, and was now coping with the aftereffects of a bone marrow transplant. In addition, the Hamilton family had been rocked with scandal. If the front-page headlines in the *Davis Landing Observer*—the town's other daily paper—were to be believed, Jeremy Hamilton, vice president of Hamilton Media, wasn't Wallace's son. Since that story had broken, Jeremy had resigned, and the reins of the company had been passed to Tim Hamilton, the next oldest son. Betty at the Bakeshoppe, where Bryan had stopped for a quick cup of coffee before his interview, had told him that news—and also that the youngest Hamilton daughter, Melissa, had run off with her boyfriend. It seemed wealth didn't insulate people from problems. Even the mighty Hamiltons were vulnerable to scandal and sorrow.

The elevator came to a stop, and the knot in Bryan's stomach cinched tighter as the door slid open to reveal a slim, attractive woman with huge brown eyes and long russet hair, dressed in a flowing floral skirt and soft knit top. She looked vaguely familiar, but only when she tucked a strand of hair behind her ear in a familiar, nervous gesture did he recognize the beauty before him as Heather Hamilton.

"Heather?"

An anxious smile tugged at the corners of her mouth. "Guilty."

Exiting the elevator, he extended his hand. "I almost didn't recognize you. You've grown up."

Shifting her notebook from one arm to the other, she returned his handshake. "I was nineteen when you left," she reminded him. "I was already grown up."

"Okay. Let me rephrase that. You look great."

"Meaning I didn't before?"

Her teasing response and the twinkle in her eye couldn't quite mask the insecure undertone in her voice. Bryan recalled that her self-esteem had never been too high. Thanks in part, he supposed, to living in Amy's shadow. Her sister had been the golden girl. With her long blond hair, sky-blue eyes, porcelain skin and fabulous figure, it was no wonder that Amy had headed the cheerleading squad and been elected homecoming queen. The fact that she'd excelled at school as well and was the editor of the yearbook made her an even more formidable role model for her younger sisters. But he was glad to see that Heather seemed to have come into her own.

"You always looked great," Bryan countered.

Grinning, Heather shook her head. "Nice try. But I could never compete on the looks front with…" She pulled herself up short. "Well, let's just say that my natural assets benefited from a recent makeover courtesy of *Nashville Living* when our makeover-of-the-month subject left us high and dry at the last minute."

As they talked, she led him through a sea of cubicles toward an enclosed conference room. Heather took a seat at the head of the long table, and gestured to a chair at a right angle to hers. "Make yourself comfortable. Amy will join us in a moment. Can I get you some coffee?"

"No, thanks. I already indulged at Betty's Bakeshoppe." He set his portfolio on the table and pulled out his chair, resisting a strong temptation to reach up and loosen his tie, which seemed to be growing tighter by the second. Suits had never been his attire of choice, and he wore them only on rare occasions.

"We were very impressed with your credentials, Bryan. It sounds like you've been busy since you left Davis Landing. How did you end up in Missouri?"

A shadow crossed his face as he took his seat. "My wife grew up there. Since her mother was a widow, and not in the best of health, we decided to stay close after we got married."

A soft look stole over Heather's face. "I heard about your wife. I'm so sorry, Bryan."

"Thank you. It's been hard. But my son, Dylan, doesn't give me a chance to sit around feeling sorry for myself. Five-year-olds have more energy than the Hoover Dam and more questions than Barbara Walters."

Chuckling, Heather leaned back in her chair. "I imagine you have plenty of ideas for a column on family issues."

A wry grin tugged at the corners of his lips. "I could write a book. Being a single dad has been—"

The words died in his throat as his gaze flickered over Heather's shoulder. She didn't even need to turn to know that Amy had arrived. The tense muscles in her shoulders eased and she breathed a sigh of relief. She'd half expected her sister to cancel at the last minute. Despite Amy's declaration that Bryan didn't mean anything to her anymore, Heather knew that she'd been shaken by the prospect of his reappearance. She wouldn't have been surprised to get a message saying that Amy had been called into an emergency meeting with Typhoon Tim—a nickname bestowed on their brother by the staff since he'd taken over the reins at Hamilton Media. True to his Type A personality, he'd made it clear that the company wasn't going to miss a beat because of the change in command, and he'd been on a whirlwind fact-finding mission to each department, often leaving chaos in his wake. Amy had been called into more meetings in the past four weeks than she'd attended in the past four years, as she'd grumbled to Heather on more than one occasion. So she could have used that as an excuse to cancel out on today's interview. But to her credit, she'd shown up.

As Amy paused in the doorway, Bryan took his time rising, trying to reconcile the woman ten paces away with the girl he'd once loved. She was just as blonde. Just as stunning. Just as poised and elegant and self-confident as she'd been back in those heady days when they were in love. Or when *he'd* been in love, he corrected himself. In retrospect, he wasn't sure her feelings had ever been as strong as his. But he hadn't been wrong about his assessment of her beauty then. And he wasn't wrong now.

In high school, Amy had worn her hair long. Now it was shoulder length, curling under slightly on her shoulders and parted a bit to one side. She was just as trim and toned as ever, and her dark teal suit and matching sling-back pumps were fashionable without being trendy. Her slim skirt revealed a discreet length of shapely leg, and the short jacket called attention to her small waist. The self-confidence she'd exhibited in high school had been a mere preview of the powerful presence she now radiated in her executive position. If he thought he detected a slight tremble in her hand, if her smile looked a bit forced, if a flash of pain seemed to dart across her eyes when she looked at him, he chalked it up to the awkwardness of the situation. This wasn't comfortable for either of them. They had too much history.

While Bryan did his quick assessment, Amy did hers. She'd recognize Bryan anywhere, of course. His distinctive auburn hair and quiet demeanor hadn't changed. And he still looked as fit and lean as ever. In fact, if anything, he'd grown more attractive with age. Maturity suited him. Made him even more appealing.

An unexpected quiver raced up Amy's

spine, and for a brief second the years melted away as the memory of their first kiss, beside the lake in Sugar Tree Park, flashed vividly across her mind. As if it had been yesterday, she recalled the way his deep green eyes had softened and warmed, inviting her to look into his soul as he searched her face before touching his lips to hers in a tender, almost reverent, kiss. Now, as their gazes met, she wondered if he, too, was remembering the sweet, heady joy of that moment. But it was impossible to tell. His shuttered eyes reflected wariness, and there was a disillusionment in their depths that had never been there before. It seemed that whatever fascination she had once held for him had long since disappeared. She'd expected that, of course. Yet somewhere deep in her heart, it hurt to have that fact confirmed. But that was her problem. And today wasn't about them, or the past, anyway. It was about business, and tomorrow. A fact she'd do well to remember.

Forcing her lips to maintain their forced smile, she moved into the room and extended her hand. "Hello, Bryan. Welcome."

"Thank you." His clasp was firm, sure—and brief.

Taking her seat across from him, Amy

turned to Heather. Her sister had gotten her into this, and Amy intended to let her take the lead. "Heather, why don't you explain the position to Bryan, since it will report to you."

As Heather spoke, Amy was content to observe. Her sister did a fine job outlining the job, and Bryan asked all the appropriate questions. When Heather finished, Amy suggested that Bryan walk them through his portfolio.

While they reviewed a number of the stories and columns Bryan had written, Amy let Heather ask most of the questions. When they reached the last page, Heather turned to her. "Is there anything else you need to see?"

"No. That should do it."

"Okay. We're interviewing three candidates, Bryan. I'm hoping we'll be able to make a decision by the end of the week. Have you moved back to town yet?"

"Yes. Until I get settled, Dylan and I are living with my dad." He jotted a number on the tablet in front of him, tore off the sheet and handed it to Heather. "If you have any other questions, don't hesitate to call."

After tucking the sheet into her notebook, Heather stood. "We will. Thank you for coming in today."

Rising, he zipped his portfolio closed and

reached out to shake hands with her. "I appreciate the opportunity." For most of the interview, he'd focused on Heather, looking at Amy only when he couldn't avoid it. He was well aware that she hadn't said much, nor asked many questions.

Now, after a brief hesitation, he transferred his attention to the woman who had once stolen his heart, then trampled on it. The quick glimpse of regret in her unguarded eyes jolted him, but it was gone so fast he was sure he'd imagined it. Amy Hamilton had never regretted anything. She'd always been decisive in her choices, wasting no time on second guesses or looking back. He'd admired that confidence years ago, assuming it was a result of being an oldest daughter who had been raised in a life of privilege.

Her poised self-confidence was still very much in evidence as she returned his look. Yet it had changed in some subtle way, he realized. Where once it had been brash and certain, it now seemed tempered by humility. As if she'd learned a few hard lessons along the road of life, had discovered that even the confident sometimes make mistakes. That life itself held no certainties. That all the money and power and prestige in the world couldn't shield a person from heartache. And the Hamiltons had had plenty of heartache in the past few months.

As he reached out to take the hand she extended, he was tempted for one brief instant to feel sorry for Amy Hamilton. Once upon a time, in the days before life had buffeted him with a succession of harsh blows, back when his faith had been strong, he would have given in to that temptation. But the compassion and charity that had once filled his heart had vanished, leaving an empty void in their place. Just Dylan and his dad, along with his brother and his family, could touch his heart. They were the only ones he let get close. It was safer that way. Caring about others, loving them, led to hurt. As the woman standing across from him well knew. If she cared. Or even remembered.

Not that it mattered, of course. Amy Hamilton meant nothing to him anymore. If he got the job, fine. He would enjoy working with Heather. If he didn't…well, something else would come along. It had to. Because losing his job had been the final blow. He'd endured all the loss and disappointment he could take.

As he followed Heather back to the elevator,

a sense of defeat and discouragement suddenly weighed down his shoulders. With no other prospects, he *did* need this job. Although it had been a long time since he'd prayed, a long time since he'd done anything but blame God for taking his wife far too soon, he needed help now. Since he didn't know where else to turn, he spoke in the silence of his heart.

Lord, You haven't done me many favors lately. To be honest, I'm not even sure why I'm talking to You now. But I don't know where else to go for help. I need this job. Or some job. I want to provide for Dylan, to give him the best life I can. But I can't do that without some source of income. This isn't the job I would have chosen. I'd prefer to stay far away from the Hamiltons. But I can deal with it— for Dylan's sake. Please, Lord…just give me the chance. Please.

Chapter Two

Amy raised her mug to her lips and let the hot liquid slide down her throat. She needed something to settle her churning stomach, but so far the coffee wasn't doing the trick. Nor had she helped the problem by skipping breakfast. Eating hadn't been an option, though. The mere thought of food had made her queasy.

Under normal circumstances, she'd be worried about feeling ill, considering that she never got sick. But the circumstances were anything but normal. Today, Bryan Healey was joining the staff of *Nashville Living*. Not as a freelance columnist, but as a full-time employee.

Grimacing, Amy set her cup back on her desk with more force than necessary, sloshing brown liquid onto the polished mahogany surface. Disgusted, she reached for some tissue in her desk drawer and sopped up the mess. If she was this rattled before Bryan even started, how was she going to cope with his presence every day?

As she swiped at the puddle, her thoughts were as dark as the sodden tissue in her hand. In her gut, she felt this was a mistake. Yet, after interviewing all three candidates, it had been clear that Bryan was far and away the best qualified. After much soul searching, Amy had reconciled herself to offering him the free-lance job. Then Heather had come to her with the news that one of their most-seasoned feature writers had turned in her resignation because her husband had been transferred. And she'd suggested that they combine that job with the freelance family-columnist position and offer it to Bryan, giving him a much higher income—and benefits.

Heather's proposal had been logical. And short of admitting to her sister that she found Bryan's presence disruptive, there had been no alternative but to tell her to extend an offer. Amy's faint hope that Bryan would turn it down had been quickly dashed when he'd accepted the same day.

The good news was that she wouldn't have to deal with him one-on-one. Heather would be his boss. The only time their paths would have to cross was at weekly staff meetings—like today. And once they got past the initial awkwardness, things would be fine, she reassured herself. It had just been a shock seeing him the first time. After all, she was an adult. She could cope with this. She ran a magazine, didn't she? Dealt with dozens of crises every day? The reappearance of an old boyfriend shouldn't cause too many problems. And if it did, she'd just plunge even more deeply into her work, which had provided a great refuge for her during the past eight years. If some thought she was a workaholic…well, so be it. Keeping busy had always helped her survive when life got crazy. Something it had been doing more and more in recent weeks.

As if to underscore that point, she caught sight of Tim barreling toward her, threading his way through the maze of cubicles that occupied most of the second floor. Tall, with dark, wavy hair and intense eyes, he looked like a man with a mission as he bore down on her. Considering how impeccable he always was about his custom-tailored clothing, the fact that his tie was a bit askew did not bode well. Now what? Amy wondered in dismay.

She didn't have to wait long to find out. Tim strode into her office, shut the door, planted his fists on his hips and gave her a furious look. "Are you ready for this? Jeremy is leaving town."

"What?" The shock on her face was echoed in her voice.

"You heard me. He's going off to find his *roots*." Sarcasm dripped off the last word.

"How do you know?"

"Mom called to tell me. He spoke with her last night before taking off for parts unknown."

Struggling to remain calm, Amy tried for a reasonable tone of voice. "He's upset, Tim. He's angry, and he feels betrayed. How would you like to be told that your father isn't your father? That the man who's groomed you to be his successor, who you've loved with all your heart, isn't even a blood relative?"

For a second, Tim's anger dissipated. "Okay, I'll admit it's a tough break. But of all times to leave… Dad hasn't even been out of isolation for that long. It's still touch-and-go with the transplant, and he's already worried about Hamilton Media. He doesn't need any more stress."

Amy thought about how pale her father looked each night when she stopped at the hospital to visit, his anxiety about the family business apparent as he plied her with questions. He was under more than enough pressure already. "I agree. So let's not tell him."

With a frustrated sigh, Tim raked his fingers through his hair. "That's what Mom said."

"She's right."

"Then who am I supposed to go to if I have a problem with the newspaper? Jeremy's gone, and I can't ask Dad without raising suspicion." All at once, his shoulders slumped and his voice grew disheartened, reminding Amy of the little boy he had once been, always striving to compete with his older brother yet never able to live up to his own lofty standards. "I don't want to mess things up and disappoint Dad."

Because they were so much alike, Amy knew how much that admission had cost Tim. Both high achievers, both driven, both perfectionists, both always striving to please their father, neither had ever handled setbacks or failure well. And neither liked to expose any vulnerability, to show any sign of weakness. Through her faith, Amy had discovered that it was okay to admit that she didn't have all the answers. And she'd found a way to temper her sometimes unrealistic expectations, to cut herself—and others—some slack. Tim hadn't learned that lesson yet. She prayed that someday he would. In the meantime, he needed a pep talk.

"Things will work out, Tim," she reassured him in a firm, quiet voice. "You're smart and you're conscientious. You'll make this work. And you know you have the support of the whole family. We'll help however we can. If we stick together, we'll get through this. The Hamiltons are made of strong stuff."

For a few seconds, he stared at her. Then he expelled a slow breath and straightened his shoulders. "Right. Okay. We won't tell Dad. And I worked on the *Dispatch* when I was in college. I just need to get up to speed." His usual confidence was returning with amazing speed. The matter settled, he swung around and headed for Amy's door. He was almost out when her voice stopped him.

"One more thing." He turned mid-stride to look at her, one eyebrow raised. "Ease up a little on the staff, okay? They're starting to duck when you pass by."

"I haven't been *that* bad."

Rolling her eyes, she shook her head. "Trust me. You've been that bad. Poor Dawn was almost in tears the other day. You'll be looking for another administrative assistant if you don't change your ways."

At least that seemed to get his attention. A flicker of panic flashed across his face. "I can't afford to lose her right now."

"And I can't afford to lose *anyone*. A word to the wise. Try being nice. You remember that word, don't you? *Nice*. It goes a long way."

"I have a business to run. I can't afford to waste time on niceties right now. We'll give everyone a bonus at Christmas to thank them for their patience through all this turmoil."

"You can't afford *not* to be nice. And dollars don't build loyalty or longevity or commitment in employees."

"They can't hurt." His pager began to vibrate, and he reached for it, then gave the message a rapid scan. "Gotta run. See you later."

As Amy watched him hurry away, she shook her head again. One of these days, she hoped someone would find a way to tame Typhoon Tim. But it sure wasn't going to be her. Sisters just didn't have that kind of power—even when they really did know best!

The staff meeting had gone well. Amy had let Heather introduce Bryan, and as the group had tossed around story ideas for upcoming issues, he'd jumped right in, impressing her with his suggestions. He'd always had good instincts, and it was clear that time hadn't changed that. If anything, they'd been honed through the years, seasoned with experience and polished with practice. She'd particularly liked his idea about a story on separation anxiety...in *parents*. It was a unique twist on a familiar topic, and with his only child starting kindergarten in two days, he could write with authority on the subject.

As the meeting wound down, Amy stood. "I think that wraps things up, unless there are any other issues we need to discuss?" When no one spoke, she reached for her notepad. "Okay. The pizza should be here any minute, so don't wander too far. Although I don't think I've ever had to twist anyone's arm to take advantage of a free meal."

Her comment elicited some chuckles, and as everyone gathered up their papers and rose, Amy turned to Heather. "Would you check with Herman? The pizza should have been delivered by now."

"No problem."

This was the part of the meeting Amy had been dreading. After regular sessions, the staff just dispersed. But Amy had started a practice of welcoming new employees with a casual lunch after their first staff meeting. If she skipped the custom this time, it would raise questions—which she didn't need or want. Better to act as if this was any other welcome party. Meaning she had to stick around, mingle, chat with the new employee. The thing to do was talk business, she counseled herself. Stay away from personal topics.

Steeling herself, she walked over to the tub of soft drinks on a side table and chose a diet soda. Out of the corner of her eye, she noted that Bryan was talking with a couple of other writers in the far corner. Good. As long as they kept him occupied, she could lay low. And once the pizza arrived, she'd grab a piece, say a few words to Bryan and disappear.

"Pizza's here!" Heather called from the doorway, juggling several large flat boxes. As she spread them out on the conference table, the staff converged like hungry buzzards. All except Bryan, Amy realized. He was still standing off to the side, one shoulder propped against the wall, his hands in the pockets of his khaki slacks. As if sensing her perusal, he angled his head her direction and looked at her. Short of being rude, she saw little option but to join him. Better to get it over with, anyway.

As she walked toward him, he straightened up. With her heels adding three inches to her five-foot, five-inch height, Amy was only two or three inches shorter than Bryan. As a result, she didn't have to look up very far to get a good view into his deep green eyes. Though cool and dispassionate now, Amy recalled with a pang how they had once radiated warmth and devotion. The contrast produced an almost physical ache in her heart, one she didn't intend to dwell on. It was obvious that Bryan had gotten over her long ago. And she had no one to blame for that except herself.

Looking back, she knew that her cavalier assumption that he would wait around until she was ready to make a commitment had been arrogant and insensitive. She'd known how much family meant to him, how much he wanted to establish a home of his own. But she'd selfishly disregarded his needs, his hopes and dreams. Maybe if they'd talked, they could have found a compromise. Instead, Amy had expected him to dance to her music. Even when he'd stopped calling, she'd just assumed he was giving her the space she'd asked for. His profession of love had been so ardent, so sincere, that it had never occurred to her that he was giving his heart to someone else.

By the time she'd realized what she'd lost, it had been too late. He'd been committed to another, and pride had kept her from contacting him. End of story. Or so she'd thought—until his résumé had crossed her desk. Now he was back, stirring up the embers of the flame that had once burned in her heart for him. And she had no idea how to deal with it.

She stopped beside him and tried for a smile, hoping that her inner turmoil wasn't reflected on her face. "So…did you find the meeting helpful?" Her tone was a little too bright, and the speculative look on his face told her that he'd noticed.

"It was a good chance to get a feel for everyone's working style. I'm glad you came over. I wanted to thank you for offering me the job."

"It was Heather's decision."

"But not without your stamp of approval, I'm sure."

Since she couldn't refute that, she remained silent.

Glancing over her shoulder, he lowered his voice. "I hope this isn't too awkward for you."

Jolted by his direct approach, Amy stared at him. But she supposed she shouldn't be surprised. Bryan never had been one to dance around issues. Put the problem on the table, deal with it and move on. That had always been his philosophy. And still was, it seemed.

"Not really," she responded, carefully lifting one shoulder in an indifferent shrug. "Our history is…ancient. A lot of things have happened since then. And we've both moved on with our lives."

"True." His gaze flickered to her ringless left hand, which had a death grip on the notebook she was clutching to her chest. "I hear you've never gotten married."

His unexpected comment threw her for a second, but she made a quick recovery. "No time. Work has been pretty all-consuming."

A sardonic smile touched the corners of his mouth. "You always did have more important things to do."

That hurt. Especially since he was right. Back in college, when she'd planned to take the publishing world by storm, the only thing on her radar screen had been her career. But her priorities were different now, even if Bryan had no way of knowing that. Or of knowing that her workaholic style was an escape from loneliness.

Some of her hurt must have been reflected on her face, because Bryan's expression shifted, as if he was sorry he'd made that

comment. But before he could speak, Ethan
Danes loped over to them, his camera equipment slung over his shoulder as he juggled
two pieces of pizza and a can of soda. Tall and
rangy, his sparkling eyes crackling with
energy, it was no wonder he'd been the
Hamilton Media heartthrob until he'd lost his
heart to Heather six months after his arrival at
Nashville Living.

"Have you thought about how you want to
illustrate that piece on separation anxiety?
Because if you haven't, I've got some ideas."
He took a huge bite of pizza and shifted his
cameras into a more comfortable position.

Amy welcomed the distraction. She didn't
want to venture into personal territory with
Bryan. It would be safer to confine their conversations to business. "By all means, tell us,"
she encouraged.

"It's a column, right? First person?" At
Bryan's nod, he continued. "Okay, how about
we take some pictures of you getting your son
ready for his first day of school? Maybe
giving him breakfast, packing his knapsack,
dropping him off? Readers like that personal
touch. It puts a face on the issue."

Faint furrows appeared on Bryan's brow.
"I'm not sure I want Dylan in the spotlight."

"He'll probably get a kick out of it. Unless you think the whole experience of going to school is stressful enough already."

"No. He's been in day care for years. Kindergarten won't be much of a problem for either of us. He's a little nervous about dealing with new people and a new school, but I dealt with the separation anxiety issue a long time ago."

The traumatic memory hadn't faded, however. As if it was yesterday, he recalled how it had just about ripped his heart out to drop his infant son at day care the first few weeks, after all they'd been through together. Born eight weeks early, tipping the scale a whisper above three pounds, Dylan had spent weeks in the neonatal intensive-care unit, much of the time on a ventilator. And it hadn't been smooth sailing. Twice there had been setbacks, and Bryan had raced to the hospital in the middle of the night. As he'd stood in helpless vigil beside Dylan's crib during those crises, his heart pounding, his vision blurred with tears, Dylan would look up at him with those huge, solemn brown eyes. Then his son would reach out his tiny hand and grasp Bryan's finger with a surprisingly strong grip, as if to say, *I'm going to make it, Dad. Don't worry*. And he had. But that had been the loneliest, most emotionally wrenching time in Bryan's life. Not only had he lost the wife he'd loved, but he'd awakened every day to the fear that he would also lose the son she'd died trying to save. So leaving him at day care had been the toughest thing Bryan had ever done.

"Look, I can come up with something else. No big deal."

At the sound of Ethan's voice, Bryan pulled himself back from the past. Amy's pensive expression told him that his face had revealed too much. Most of the time, he had his emotions under control. But for some reason he'd slipped up today.

"No. It's not a bad idea." He tried for a casual tone. "And you're right. Dylan would probably enjoy it. Besides, it might get his mind off the fact that he's going to be starting a new school and meeting a lot of new people."

"What do you think, Amy?"

Still struggling to get a handle on the pain that had gripped Bryan's eyes a few seconds before, it took her a moment to switch gears and respond to Ethan's question. "Um…yeah, I think it's a good idea."

"Do you want to art direct the shoot?"

She often did that. Ethan was great, but she had a good feel for composition, too, and for important pieces she often went along to provide a second opinion. While the introduction of a new columnist qualified the story as important, she knew Ethan could handle it. At the same time, she was curious to meet the little boy, after the expression she'd just seen on Bryan's face. Still, if she wanted to remain aloof from Bryan, meeting his son wouldn't be her smartest move. She needed to think this through. "I'll check my schedule and let you know. Meanwhile, you two can work out the details. Good to have you on board, Bryan."

Her welcome was perfunctory. As was Bryan's response.

"Glad to be here."

As she turned away and headed toward the door, Heather's voice stopped her on the threshold.

"Amy! Don't you want some pizza?"

Without breaking stride, Amy tossed a response over her shoulder. "I'm not that hungry. And I have another meeting to go to."

Okay, so the meeting wasn't for two hours, she acknowledged as she strode away. The part about not being hungry was true, though. Her appetite had vanished after her encounter with Bryan. Still, she'd expected the first conversation to be strained. Maybe even traumatic. But it would get easier.

Wouldn't it?

"Adorable" was the only word she could think of to describe Dylan Healey. From her position near the school entrance, Amy watched Bryan and Dylan get out of their car, then wait for Ethan to find a parking spot and join them. As she walked toward them, she studied the little boy. His tousled auburn hair was the same hue as his dad's, and he looked healthy and robust. Although his backpack, decorated with superhero cartoon figures, was all little boy, his horn-rimmed glasses gave him a studious and grown-up air. When she drew close he turned toward her, and she noted that he had Bryan's green eyes, as well as an endearing sprinkling of freckles across his nose.

The little boy tugged on Bryan's sleeve. "Hey, Dad, is that the lady you said was going to meet us here?"

Raising his head, Bryan looked in her direction. "Yeah." As she closed the remaining distance between them, Bryan dropped a protective hand to his son's shoulder. "Dylan, this is Ms. Hamilton. She's in charge of the magazine where I work. Amy, this is my son, Dylan."

It had been years since Amy had had much contact with children, and she felt a bit awkward as Dylan stared up at her, his expression solemn, as if he was trying to figure out whether he liked her or not. Adults did the same thing when they met new people, of course, but children were much more blatant in their assessment. For some reason, Amy wanted to pass muster with this little boy. Relying on her instincts, she dropped down to his level and smiled.

"Hello, Dylan."

"Hi."

"Are you excited about school?"

"I guess. Dad says I'll like it. Grandpa does, too."

"You'll meet lots of new friends."

"My dad is my best friend."

Touched, Amy smiled. "I bet he feels the same way."

"Do you have a little boy?"

A pang of regret tugged at her heart. "No."

"Don't you like kids?"

"Of course. Someday I might have a little boy or a little girl."

He considered that. "Then you'd be a mommy, right?"

She tried to swallow past the lump in her

throat. If she'd accepted the gift of love Bryan had offered her years ago, she already would be. This little one could have been hers. "Yes."

"I used to have a mommy. She lives in heaven now."

His matter-of-fact response didn't lessen the emotional impact of his words. Amy's face softened, and she was tempted to reach out and brush one of the unruly locks of hair off his forehead. Instead, she forced her lips into a smile. "I'm sure she still loves you very much." And then, feeling out of her depth in this kind of discussion, she changed the subject. "I like your backpack."

"Dad got it for me." He directed an adoring look up Bryan. "He said we'd be doing important stuff in kindergarten, and that he wanted me to bring it home in this to show him."

When she ventured a glance upward, the tender, loving look on Bryan's face as he watched his son made Amy's breath catch in her throat, and she blinked away the sting of unexpected tears. His expression reminded her of the way he had once looked at her, with profound love and absolute devotion. If Dylan idolized his father, it was clear that the feeling was mutual. The love between father and son was so strong, so potent, that Amy felt awed in its presence.

Bryan shifted his attention to her, and for a second he seemed thrown by whatever he saw on her face. But when Ethan came up beside them, the mood shifted.

"Sorry. I got hung up behind a stalled car. Hi, Amy."

She took her time rising, buying herself a few seconds to regain her composure. "How did things go at the house?" She'd begged off joining Ethan at Bryan's father's house, unwilling to get that up close and personal.

"Great. It shouldn't take us long to wrap up here."

They got down to business, and in short order Ethan had taken a series of photos of Bryan and Dylan arriving, walking into the school, saying goodbye. Amy offered a few suggestions, but Ethan, as usual, needed little direction. It was Amy, however, who noticed the opportunity for the most poignant photo of all.

"Ethan, take one more. Use the telephoto, and get the school in the background," she said in a low voice, motioning toward Bryan as the photographer began to store his equipment in his SUV. During the entire photo shoot, Bryan had been upbeat with Dylan, kidding him, laughing with him, encouraging him. Now the mood had changed. He'd opened the driver-side door of his car, propped one elbow on the roof and rested his chin on his wrist. His other hand was in his pocket, and he was staring toward the school with a pensive, melancholy expression that tugged at Amy's heart.

Without commenting, Ethan switched lenses and clicked off a series of shots, unobtrusively changing angles and positions each time. When he finished, he rejoined her. "That may be the best stuff we did. The expression on his face is priceless."

Directing her attention back toward Bryan, Amy could only agree. It was clear that this parting from Dylan was hard on him, no matter what he'd said after the staff meeting. It was just as clear that he was doing a stellar job as a single dad. Although Amy didn't know the details of his wife's death, Dylan seemed to be coping fine without a mom, thanks to Bryan. But that didn't surprise her. Bryan had always been the type to rise to the occasion, quietly stepping in to do what needed to be done.

A memory from high school surfaced, one she hadn't thought of in years. There'd been

a fire in the computer lab, and Amy—as
yearbook editor—had been most affected. Her
final files had sustained serious damage.
They'd represented weeks of work, and she'd
been panicked, distraught and frenzied. Until
Bryan had stepped forward to help.

Prior to that, Amy hadn't said more than a
dozen words to the quiet, soft-spoken senior
who had been destined to steal her heart—
and who, he later confessed, had been
carrying a torch for her since their sophomore
year. Their paths had crossed a few times
during the first half of their senior year, since
he was the editor of the school newspaper, but
only when he came to her rescue did she really
notice him. He'd spent every evening for the
next week—surviving on high-caffeine
soda—helping her to salvage what she could,
even as he tried to keep up with the demands
of his classes and his duties as newspaper
editor. As she'd discovered, he was the kind
of guy you could count on. Dylan was lucky
to have him for a father. And the woman he'd
married had been lucky to have him as a
husband, Amy acknowledged.

"How about we stop at the Bakeshoppe? I
didn't have time for breakfast this morning,
and I don't think Bryan did, either. He fixed

oatmeal and scrambled eggs for Dylan, but he didn't eat anything himself."

Ethan's voice interrupted her thoughts, and Amy turned back to him. It would be safer if she sent the two men for a meal and headed back to her office. And far more conducive to her peace of mind. She was just about to suggest that when Bryan looked her way. His bleak expression and the grooves at the corners of his mouth told her just how hard the parting had been for him. Sensing his aloneness, she wanted to do her part to help him over this hurdle.

"Sounds good to me. I'll meet you guys there."

As Amy walked back to her car, she wondered if she was making a mistake. Bryan had only been at the magazine for a few days, and their contact had been limited, but already her long-buried feelings were bubbling up, like boiling water from a covered pot. Still, given the look on his face just now, spending a little time with him seemed like the compassionate thing to do.

But she wasn't sure it was the smart thing.

Chapter Three

Ethan and Bryan were already ensconced in a booth at Betty's Bakeshoppe by the time Amy arrived. Although the popular eatery was crowded as usual, the two men had managed to snag one of the small niches. But she noted with dismay that Ethan had brought his precious camera equipment in with him instead of dropping it in his office at Hamilton Media across the street. It now occupied the seat next to him. Meaning she'd have to sit beside Bryan.

For a second her step faltered. They hadn't seen her yet. She could still make a quick escape, use some excuse about a crisis at the office. But just then Ethan caught sight of her and waved. Too late. With a sinking feeling, she urged her feet forward. Bryan eased over in the booth as she approached, giving her as much space as possible. Almost as if he didn't want to be any closer to her than necessary, Amy thought with a hollow feeling in the pit of her stomach. Sliding onto the bench, she stayed as close to the edge as she could.

"Did you order yet?" she asked, striving for a casual tone.

"No. We waited for you." Ethan handed her a menu, then motioned over her shoulder. A few seconds later, Betty appeared.

"My now, isn't this like old times." The owner whipped out her order pad and turned her attention to Amy and Bryan, her eyes twinkling. "Seems to me your favorite order used to be hot-fudge sundaes, but I expect you'd rather have something else for breakfast."

A hot flush crept up Amy's neck, and she stole a look at Ethan, who was watching the exchange with amused interest. From his expression, it was clear that Heather had filled him in on the history between Amy and Bryan.

"I think I'll just have some toast and tea, Betty." Amy handed her unopened menu back to the owner.

Betty tucked it under her arm and gave Amy a concerned look. "Aren't you feeling well?"

"I'm fine."

"You always order an omelet for breakfast."

Gritting her teeth, Amy prayed that the flush on her neck wouldn't work its way up to her cheeks. "I'm not that hungry today."

"Humph." Betty made a notation on the order pad. "How about you, Bryan?"

"Coffee. Black. And scrambled eggs."

"What about some bacon or sausage? Maybe a pancake or two? And you know our cinnamon rolls are to die for."

"Not today, thanks."

"Humph." Again, she scribbled on her notepad. "Ethan?"

"A three-egg omelet with ham and mush-rooms, a side order of country potatoes and a biscuit. Oh, and coffee with lots of cream."

"Now that's what I call a breakfast." Betty nodded her approval as she jotted down the order, then stuck her pencil in among the strands of brown and gray hair that were woven into a bun on the back of her head. "Coffee and tea will be right out. Amy, you better slide yourself in a little or you're going to end up on the floor."

As Betty hustled away, Amy lost her battle to keep the warm color from invading her face. It surged onto her cheeks, intensifying as she risked a peek at Bryan and found him watching her with an unreadable expression as she eased in an inch or two. Ethan, on the other hand, seemed amused by the whole thing, and she glared at him across the table.

Clearing his throat, the photographer had the good grace—and the good sense—to change the subject. "So…Dylan is a cute kid, Bryan. But being a father must be a challenge. I admit I've been giving it a lot of thought since Heather and I got engaged. To be honest, raising a family wasn't one of my top priorities until I met her. But it's amazing how love can change your perspective. Still, the responsibility of that whole parenting thing kind of blows my mind."

Betty deposited their mugs and joined right in on the conversation. She'd been in Davis Landing so long that she knew everyone—and felt like part of their families. "You'll be a natural, Ethan. Don't you worry about it. Just love your kids. That's the main thing. And you bring that son of yours in here soon." Betty directed her last comment to Bryan. "Get him one of those hot-fudge sundaes you and Amy used to like. My treat for his first visit."

"I'll do that. Thanks." Bryan watched her leave, then turned back to Ethan. "Betty's right. Love is the best thing you can give your kids. Just let them know that they come first in your life, and that you're on their side. My dad and mom did that with my brother and me, and I'm trying to follow their example with Dylan. It's a little harder when there's just one of you, though." A shadow passed over his face, and he reached for his mug and took a sip of coffee.

"Heather told me you'd lost your wife," Ethan sympathized. "I'm sorry. Was it very long ago?"

"Five and a half years."

Twin furrows appeared on Amy's brow, and she turned to him for the first time since Betty had deposited their drinks. "How old is Dylan?"

"Five and a half." As Ethan and Amy stared at him, Bryan answered the unspoken question suspended in the silence. "Darlene had a condition known as preeclampsia. It's not an uncommon complication of pregnancy, and most of the time it's mild. Hers wasn't. In its most severe form, it can endanger the mother and put the child at risk. There's no cure except delivering the baby, and timing is everything. Ours was off. Darlene suffered a cerebral hemorrhage, and Dylan was taken eight weeks early by C-section. He made it. She didn't."

Horrified, Amy stared at Bryan. His spare,

curt speech had been delivered in a clinical, dispassionate voice as he stared into the murky depths of his coffee. But his white-knuckled grip on the handle, the deep creases of strain around his mouth and the tense line of his jaw spoke of a pain and trauma undimmed by the passage of years. She wanted to say something, anything, to comfort him, but her throat was too tight to let any words through, even if she could find some that were appropriate.

Ethan seemed just as much at a loss as she was. As they exchanged a What-do-we-say-now? look, Betty came to their rescue and deposited their plates on the table.

"Here you go. Ethan, I put a packet of honey on your plate. I know you like that with your biscuits. Bryan, I had Justine add a little parsley to those scrambled eggs. Dresses them up quite a bit. Amy, here's a little cinnamon-sugar mixture for that toast. I remember you used to like that as a little girl. I like it myself. Turns plain toast into comfort food. Can I get you folks anything else?"

Ethan found his voice. "No, thanks. This looks good, Betty."

"Just give me or one of the girls a wave if you need something. Eat up."

As Amy stared down at her plate of toast, she doubted whether she'd be able to choke down more than a few bites after listening to Bryan's sad story. Maybe the cinnamon sugar would help. But as for turning the toast into comfort food…not today. It would take more than that homey recipe to ease the ache in her heart that Bryan's story had produced.

He stirred beside her, and she heard the clink of cutlery against crockery as he forked a bite of egg. Ethan, bless him, had shifted the conversation to an innocuous discussion of fishing conditions on the Cumberland River, and Bryan was responding. Amy let them chat, keeping her attention focused on her plate. She didn't want to look at Bryan. Not yet. Not until she worked through the emotions his story had stirred up. Not until she felt enough in control that she could risk letting him look into her eyes without worrying that he'd see right into her heart and know that she still cared for him. That his pain had touched her far more than it could have if she'd truly moved on with her life, as she'd told him she had in the staff meeting.

At least everyone ate fast. Ethan cleaned his plate, and Bryan put a good dent in his scrambled eggs. Amy tore her toast into little pieces and clumped them in a pile, hoping no one would notice that most of it remained uneaten. However, as she slid from the booth, followed by Bryan, he gave her plate a quick scrutiny. When he stood beside her, his face just inches from hers, his green eyes were questioning, probing.

Feeling somehow exposed, Amy checked her watch. "Well, I'm off. I'll see you two back at the office. Just put this on my tab," she instructed Betty, who was passing by.

"Sure thing, hon," the owner called over her shoulder.

Then, without a backward glance at the two men, Amy headed for the exit. And tried not to run.

Leaning back in her office chair, Amy rested her elbows on the arms and steepled her fingers as she stared at her computer screen. Since breakfast two hours before, in between phone calls from the printer and an impromptu—and disruptive—visit from Typhoon Tim, she'd managed to find out an awful lot about preeclampsia by surfing the Net. And none of it was pretty. The disease could cause headaches, visual disturbances, high blood pressure, confusion, impaired liver function, seizures, kidney failure, coma—and death. And that was just in the mother. The baby could suffer slower-than-normal growth, oxygen deficiency, low birth weight, premature birth—and death. According to everything Amy had read, dilemmas arose when early delivery would solve the mother's problems but put the baby at risk of the effects of extreme prematurity.

Bryan's passing reference about his and Darlene's timing being off led Amy to believe they'd faced that very dilemma. As it was, Dylan had been born two months early—borderline for many problems, according to the Internet. But he didn't seem to suffer from any lasting effects. Except maybe the glasses. It seemed that premature children were at higher risk for eye complications. She leaned forward to read a bit more on that subject. She'd had no idea that preemies could…

"Can I interrupt for a minute?"

At the sound of Bryan's voice, Amy spun toward the door, a guilty flush suffusing her face.

"Sorry to startle you. I didn't realize you were that deep in concentration." His focus shifted to the screen behind her, and she tried to remember if the type had been large or small. In either case, she was sure he couldn't read it from the doorway. Could he?

Steeling herself, she swiveled her chair just enough to reach her keyboard. In the second before she closed her Internet connection, she saw that the headline on her screen, "Long-term Effects of Premature Birth," was more than big enough to be read from across the room. Closing her eyes, she took a deep breath and caught her lower lip in her teeth. She couldn't keep her back to him forever. She might as well turn and face the music. Praying he'd let it pass, she clicked out of the screen, then eased her chair around.

"No problem. I was just doing some research. What can I do for you?" She congratulated herself for sounding far calmer than she felt.

Instead of responding at once, he folded his arms and propped a shoulder against her doorway, as if debating his next move. When he spoke at last, her heart sank. "If you wanted to know anything about Dylan, you could have just asked."

Amy was used to being in control. At the magazine, at home, in her life. At least, as much as God let her be. Her self-confidence was solid, and it took a lot to fluster her. But Bryan had been doing it with almost no effort ever since his return. His mere presence was enough to throw her off balance, let alone his straightforward, cut-to-the-chase manner. She should have remembered how direct he could be when she'd agreed to hire him. At one time she'd admired that trait. Had liked his honesty, his willingness to address problems without game playing. Not anymore. Not when it put her on the hot seat.

His regard was steady as he waited for her response, and Amy forced herself to maintain eye contact as she spoke. "I didn't think it would be appropriate to ask for more information about such a personal subject. But I found Dylan charming, and after your comments this morning I wondered how rough his early start might have been for him." *And for you.* She left the latter unvoiced, however.

Again, a couple of beats of silence ensued. She wasn't sure he was even going to reply. But he did. "Pretty rough." He studied her, as if considering how to proceed. Then he inclined his head toward the door. "Do you mind if I close this?"

She shook her head, and he pushed himself away from the frame, then eased the door shut. Before she could suggest that he sit down, he strolled over to stare out of her window. It offered a scenic view of the Cumberland River, which ran through the middle of town a few blocks away. The strong midday light highlighted the faint lines around his eyes, the slight horizontal creases in his forehead, the hard line of lips that had once been supple and soft. He had changed in so many ways, Amy thought with a pang. He'd been tested by fire, and while he'd survived, he'd paid a price. Bryan had always been serious, but he'd known how to laugh, too. The flashes of spontaneous joy in his sparkling eyes, his dry wit, his ability to make lemonade out of lemons—and do it with a smile—had always appealed to her. Looking at him now, Amy suspected that joy and laughter had been absent from his life for some time. Only around Dylan did she catch a glimpse of the man he had once been. Bryan might still be doing his best to make lemonade, but the flavor of the ingredients seemed to have left a bitter taste in his mouth.

He turned to her then, and his question caught her off guard. "Why did you hire me, Amy?"

Trying to steady her fluttering pulse, she told him what she'd told herself. "You were the best qualified person for the job. Heather recommended you. I couldn't find any grounds to object."

"But you don't want me here."

"I didn't say that."

"You didn't have to. I'm picking up…unsettling…vibes."

"Maybe it's your imagination."

"I don't think so." He walked over and put his hands flat on her desk, leaning toward her, his face just inches from hers. "Look, let me just lay this on the line, okay? I know you don't want me around. I got that message a long time ago." His mouth twisted into a mirthless smile, there and gone in a flash. "Frankly, I don't want to be here, either. In fact, I wouldn't be if it wasn't for Dylan. But I need this job, Amy. At least until something else comes along. In the meantime, I'll try to stay out of your way as much as possible. I promise you that I'll put our personal history and differences aside and give the magazine a hundred and ten percent.

"Now, as for what you were looking at on the Net. That's why I need this job. After what I've been through these past six years, I know the value of insurance, and I can't afford COBRA long-term. When Dylan was born, he spent eight weeks in neonatal intensive care.

Even though he didn't suffer from starvation or severe oxygen deprivation in the womb, he had problems. He couldn't breathe on his own at first, so he was hooked up to a ventilator. Twice we almost lost him. When I was finally allowed to take him home, I was scared to death. At five pounds, he was so tiny that I didn't see how he could survive. But he did."

A muscle clenched in his jaw, and he sucked in a deep breath. "That didn't mean we were out of the woods, however. As I'm sure you discovered, premature children can have vision problems. That's why he wears glasses. And why he's already had one eye surgery. I hope that's the only one he needs. But I don't take anything for granted anymore." Bryan's eyes, intense and raw, held her captive. "Now you know Dylan's story. And why I need this job. No matter how much you dislike me, no matter how awkward it is to have me around, I ask that you try to overlook your discomfort for Dylan's sake. To have compassion for my child. In return, I'll give *Nashville Living* everything I have to offer until something else comes along. Can you do that?"

Amy was so caught up in Bryan's gripping gaze that it took several seconds for the sound of knocking to penetrate her consciousness.

By the time it did, Heather had cracked the door and was peeking in. As Bryan straightened up, her sister looked from him to Amy, then back again, her eyes widening.

"Sorry. I can come back later. I didn't realize you were…in conference."

As she started to close the door, Amy tried—and failed—to find her voice. Fortunately, Bryan had better luck. "Hang on a sec. You were the one I was looking for."

Once more, Heather's head appeared around the door. "I was?"

"Yes." Bryan moved across the room toward her, and Heather opened the door wider, flashing a still-uncertain look at Amy. "I wanted to remind you that I need to pick Dylan up at school. The first day is just a short orientation. Since you weren't here, I was going to let Amy know I'd be gone a little longer than usual over lunch."

"Oh. Right. I remember. I had to run up to Tim's office with some information he needed, and I was gone a little longer than I expected."

"No problem. I just didn't want anyone to think I was cutting out early after only a few days on the job."

He was halfway out the door before Amy found her voice. "Bryan." When he turned and looked at her, she continued. "About that other question you asked me. The answer is yes."

Did the tension in his face ease a bit, or was it just her imagination?

"Okay. Thanks."

Heather watched him go, then looked back toward Amy, making no attempt to hide the query in her eyes. Nor did she hesitate giving voice to it. "What was that all about?"

Busying herself with a stack of copy on her desk, Amy refused to meet Heather's eyes. "Bryan already told you."

"Sorry. Not buying. The atmosphere in here when I opened the door was thick enough to cut with the proverbial knife."

In recent weeks, Amy had taken great joy in watching Heather bloom. The transformation from shy caterpillar to butterfly had been amazing to witness, and Amy had been delighted when Heather began spreading her wings to soar with new confidence. Until today. Today, she wished Heather would revert to her former ways and crawl back into her cocoon the way she used to do when Amy gave her the I'm-the-boss-and-I-don't-have-time-for-this look. Instead, Heather was holding her ground, watching her sister with a speculative expression. And Amy didn't like it. Not one bit.

"Go back to work, Heather."

Folding her arms across her chest, Heather gave Amy a smug appraisal. "I get the message. Back off. The question is, why?"

"Heather…" This time there was a warning note in Amy's voice.

"Okay, okay. But why won't you tell me what's going on?"

"Because there isn't anything going on."

"Then why won't you talk about it?" At the expression on Amy's face, Heather sighed. "Fine. Have it your way. But you know what? You may be able to fool yourself, but you can't fool me. I know you too well. Whatever just happened in here rattled you. Big time."

With a flounce of her stylish, newly layered hair, Heather departed, leaving Amy relieved but not at peace. Not even close. For years she'd convinced herself that she'd dealt with the loss of Bryan. That while she might harbor feelings for him deep inside, the man who had stolen her heart once upon a time, in the distant past, had no place in her future. Reconciled to that fact, she'd done her best to go on with her life. It had never occurred to her that he'd reappear. Or that if he did, he'd disrupt her peace of mind so thoroughly.

Heather was right. Bryan rattled her big-time.

And there wasn't a thing she could do about it, short of terminating his employment. But his appeal to her sense of compassion, for Dylan's sake, had nixed that possibility. As a result, she'd best come up with another plan, pronto.

At least he didn't know the real reason his presence disturbed her, she consoled herself. He thought she just didn't want a guy she'd discarded years before hanging around. That she still wanted no part of him. And it was better that way. Safer. As long as he kept his distance, she'd be able to cope. Right?

She wanted to answer with a confident "yes." But if she looked deep in her heart, she knew that the more honest—and unsettling— answer was an uncertain "maybe."

"How did it go, champ?" Bryan grinned down at Dylan as they walked toward the car.

Dylan hoisted his backpack higher on his shoulder and beamed up at his dad. "It was awesome. Ms. Patterson is nice, and I met a bunch of other kids. Joe and Mark and Andrew. And Greg sits next to me. He wants me to come over to his house Saturday to play. Can I, Dad?"

Opening the car door, Bryan settled Dylan in his seat and verified that his belt was secure before responding. "I'll have to check with his mom and dad first. Ask him for his phone number tomorrow and I'll give them a call."

As they drove home, Bryan didn't have to do much prodding to elicit a steady and enthusiastic stream of information on the school, the students, the classroom and a dozen other topics. It seemed Dylan's starring role in the photo shoot this morning had given him instant celebrity status, smoothing his transition to the new school, just as Ethan had suggested. Bryan was just grateful that the first day had gone well. Change was always difficult for children. And it wasn't a whole lot easier for adults.

As Dylan chattered, Bryan kept half an ear on the conversation while he thought about the recent changes in his own life. If people had told him a month ago that he'd soon be employed by *Nashville Living*, he'd have laughed in their faces. Amy Hamilton had been the last person he'd ever wanted to see again, let alone work for. Yet it seemed fate had conspired to bring them together again. At one time he would have wondered if perhaps God had had a hand in it, but he didn't spend a whole lot of time thinking about the Almighty anymore. After the blows life had dealt him, he'd grown angry with the Lord, just as Jonah had. After all, how much was a man expected to take? He'd been dumped by his first love, lost his second love, spent agonizing weeks watching his son fight for his life, lost his mother to cancer…all in the space of a handful of years. If the Lord had shown him any compassion through all of his trials and tribulations, he'd missed it.

Now he had to deal with Amy. He supposed he should have bitten his tongue and kept his thoughts to himself this morning, but something had snapped when he'd caught her surfing the Net, looking for information about his son's health. What had been her motivation, anyway? Morbid curiosity? Or was she afraid that concerns about Dylan would distract him at work, that he wouldn't give Hamilton Media his full attention? She'd always put her career first; surely that had something to do with her research. She didn't waste time on things that had no payoff.

A niggling voice in his conscience told him that maybe he was being unduly harsh in his assessment, considering that she'd agreed to overlook whatever discomfort or distaste she had about his presence and let him stay until he found something else. Even after he'd confronted her this morning, overstepping the employer/employee bounds, she'd agreed to wait it out. He supposed he should be grateful. After all, as he'd told her, he needed this job.

At the same time, after only a handful of days at *Nashville Living*, he knew that the sooner he got out, the better. His comfort level with the situation was no higher than Amy's, though he thought he'd done a better job masking his unease. To be honest, he'd been surprised by the depth of his discomfort. Although he hadn't expected to enjoy working with Amy, he'd figured his overall reaction would be neutral. She was just someone he'd known—and cared about—a long time ago. But times had changed. He'd changed. He'd moved on and found someone else to love.

Thoughts of Darlene brought the whisper of a smile to his face. After giving his heart to Amy, he'd never expected to fall in love again. He'd thought his first love had been the only woman for him. Then he'd met Darlene Sweetman in a coffee shop he'd frequented on campus. Though he'd attended the Northwestern School of Journalism on a scholarship, he hadn't had the most plush accommodations. Since his quad dorm room hadn't been conducive to study, he'd taken refuge in the coffee shop to do his homework.

At first he'd paid little attention to Darlene as she came and went, refilling his coffee cup, murmuring a few words, giving him a shy smile. Dark haired and quiet, with a sweet face, she'd never been the type to call attention to herself. It had taken a nasty bout with pneumonia the fall of his senior year to make him realize that she had noticed him a lot more than he'd noticed her. When she heard he was ill, she'd brought him soup every day from the coffee shop, often staying to chat. After he expressed concern about falling behind in his studies, she'd volunteered to make copies of his teachers' notes, increasing her own heavy schedule. Over time, she'd not only caught his eye but won his heart with her gentle goodness and nurturing manner. He'd also been blown away by their compatibility. They'd shared the same values. Both had had a strong faith. Both had wanted to start a family right away.

It had taken Bryan a while to recognize the comfortable contentment he felt around Darlene as love. It had been so different from his feelings for Amy, which had been pulse pounding and exhilarating and exciting. In time, though, he'd realized that those feelings hadn't been the deepest expression of love,

but more like the attraction of a moth to a
flame. An attraction that was volatile and dangerous, that could easily burn you. As he'd
learned firsthand. His love for Darlene had
known no great highs or lows, ups or downs.
It had been steady and sure and calm. If she
hadn't delivered quite the emotional punch
that Amy had, well…he had chalked that off
to maturity, to growing up and mellowing
hormones. He had no longer been a teenager
with a crush, after all. By Easter, he and
Darlene had become engaged.

Bryan had expected to spend a life of quiet
contentment with his wife. To fill a house with
children who would add joy and fulfillment
and wonder to their days. But it had taken three
years and several miscarriages before Darlene
had achieved a viable pregnancy. How they'd
rejoiced when she'd passed the halfway mark,
as they'd watched the ultrasound monitor
together and marveled at the child sheltered
within her! And then things had changed with
a suddenness that had left them reeling. All at
once, both Darlene and their child had been in
jeopardy. Bryan's grip tightened on the
steering wheel as he recalled those nightmare
days. Days when they'd faced terrible choices
with unknown consequences. Days when…

"…really work for Ms. Hamilton?"

With a start, Bryan flicked a glance in the rearview mirror. Dylan was looking at him, his face alight with interest as he awaited his father's answer. Except Bryan wasn't sure what the question had been. Something about Amy. That much had penetrated his reverie.

"What was that, champ?"

"I asked you if you work for that lady who was at school this morning when the man took the pictures. I think you said her name was Ms. Hamilton."

"Well, mostly I work for her sister. Ms. Hamilton is the boss of the whole magazine."

"She's pretty."

Unsure how to respond, Bryan remained silent.

"She has golden hair. Don't angels have golden hair?"

His mouth twisting into a cynical smile, Bryan chose his words with care. "I've never seen an angel. But I expect some of them do have golden hair."

"She's nice, too. Do you see her every day?"

Not if I can help it. But again, his spoken words were different. "She's a pretty busy lady. Lots of times I don't see her at all."

"She liked my backpack." Dylan turned to

stare out the window. When he continued, his voice was softer. "A lot of kids' mommies came today to get them. I wish I had a mommy."

His son's comment was like a knife twisting in Bryan's gut. Since Darlene's mother had died six months before, Dylan had become more and more aware of the lack of female nurturing in his life. In her final months, Doris Sweetman's failing health had slowed her up a great deal, but she'd been a loving grandmother nonetheless. Dylan felt her loss keenly. Since her death, he'd been looking for someone to fill the empty place in his life. He'd voiced the desire for a mother on a regular basis. And Bryan always responded the same way.

"You do have a mommy, Dylan. We have her picture in the bedroom at Grandpa's house. She's in heaven now, but she still loves you." Someday he'd tell him just how much. That Darlene had died in order to give her son a better chance to live. But this wasn't the time. Not yet.

"I know. But it's not the same. I want a mommy who can cook my breakfast and tuck me in at night and tell me stories."

"You have me. I do all those things for you. Are you saying I'm not doing a good job?"

Bryan tried for a teasing tone, though it was hard to pull off.

"You do real good. But it would be nice to have a mommy, too. Then we could be a real family. Maybe someday you'll find a mommy for me, huh, Dad?"

Marry again? Bryan doubted it. He'd been there, done that. The last thing on earth he wanted to do was get involved with another woman.

"What do you think, Dad?"

"We'll see." It was an automatic response. One every kid recognized as noncommittal. And Dylan was no exception, given the disappointed look on his face, reflected in the rearview mirror. But it was the best Bryan could do.

Because both times he'd risked loving, he'd gotten hurt. If he went down a third time, he'd never come up again. And that was a chance he wasn't willing to take.

Chapter Four

"I heard from Kevin today. They're going to be able to come in for the party."

From the twinkle in his father's eye, Bryan knew the older man was pleased that his eldest son and his family were going to come home from Houston for his retirement celebration.

"That's great, Dad. And I'm glad they're giving you a good send-off. You deserve it after thirty-five years on the job. Are you going to miss working there?"

For several seconds his father regarded him across the oak table that had been a gathering place in the Healey kitchen for as long as Bryan could remember. It seemed like just yesterday that they'd all sat around its worn surface, sharing the events of their day, laughing and telling stories as they enjoyed the simple, satisfying meals prepared by Catherine Healey. This was where Bryan had come to appreciate the great gift of family, why he hadn't wanted to delay starting his own.

Much had happened in the intervening years. And the time had passed so quickly. His mother was gone now, and his father's thick, russet hair had turned white long ago, as had his bushy eyebrows. At five foot nine, he wasn't tall by modern standards, nor was he as trim as he could be. But then, his father had never been thin. *Solid* had been the way people described James Healey. *Solid* and *kind*. Bryan would also add *wise* to that list, and *strong*. James Healey's Killarney-blue eyes, set in a ruddy complexion, reflected strength as well as compassion. But Bryan had always been aware of a poignant melancholy in their depths, too. Never more so than right now.

"No, son. I won't miss a thing. It was a job. Sure, it was a good one, and I was glad to have it. I wouldn't want the good Lord to think I'm complaining. It provided us with a nice home and food on the table, but thirty-five years on an assembly line is enough. To be honest, I had hoped for better things when I came here from Ireland. I was going to make my fortune, not spend a lifetime at a car factory. But I was fresh off the farm, without even a high school education, and I learned fast enough that I wasn't going to take America by storm. Still, I suppose I did all right. I raised two fine boys and was blessed with a wonderful woman who made me feel like I was a success even if I only put headlights on cars."

Bryan's throat tightened as he gripped his mug and studied the older man across from him. Never once in all the years he was growing up had he heard his father complain, nor talk about his own dreams. He'd always just done what had to be done, putting his own hopes and needs aside. His dad's efforts may not have produced worldly treasures, like Wallace Hamilton's had, but he'd created a legacy far more valuable. He'd instilled in his children a solid work ethic, a belief that they could achieve anything they set their sights on, an understanding of the importance of family and a deep faith. That the latter had fallen into disrepair for Bryan wasn't his father's fault, even if it was a source of disappointment to the older man.

On impulse, Bryan reached across the table and laid his hand over his father's. "You were a success, Dad."

James smiled. "There's more than a wee bit of your mother in you, I'm thinking."

"I'm lucky if there is."

"That you would be. Now, tell me how the new job is going."

Shrugging, Bryan took a sip of his coffee. "Okay, I guess. I don't plan to stay there forever, just until something else comes along. In the meantime, though, I'll start looking for a house. I don't want to overextend our welcome."

"As if you could. Truth be told, it's nice to have some company. I'm enjoying the chance to get better acquainted with my grandson. Those once- or twice-a-year visits just whetted my appetite. He's a fine boy. You've done a good job with him, son."

"It's been a challenge."

"That it has, I'm sure."

"Hey, Grandpa, when are we leaving?" Dylan barreled into the kitchen, skidding to a stop beside the table. It was clear he'd tried to tame his unruly hair with a wet comb, though with limited success.

"My, now, don't you look fine, all dressed up in your Sunday best," James said.

"It *is* Sunday, Grandpa."

"So it is. And judging by that clock on the wall, we'd better get a move on or we'll miss the first song. Pastor Abernathy is a great believer in the virtue of promptness. He'll have that organ pumped up right at six o'clock." Rising, he reached for the car keys on the kitchen counter. When he spoke again, his tone was casual. "All these years of shift work, I never have been able to get to the morning services. So I haven't kept up with the Hamiltons. I hear they've had their share of trouble lately, though. How's Amy holding up? She was such a sweet girl, and I know she loves her father. This must be hard on her."

His father had always had a soft spot for Bryan's first girlfriend. When Bryan had invited her home on a number of occasions for family celebrations, she'd dazzled everyone with her charm and poise. His family had been sorry when they'd broken up. By then, Bryan had been away at school and hadn't offered much of an explanation, except that they'd grown apart. And once he got engaged, they'd never discussed Amy Hamilton again. He supposed his father had only brought her up now because she was Bryan's boss.

"I haven't talked to her about it. We don't see that much of each other."

"Who's Amy?" Dylan wiggled onto the edge of a chair and propped his chin in his hand.

"Amy Hamilton. From my office." Bryan

consulted his watch. He didn't want to talk about Amy. "Aren't you going to be late?" he prompted.

"You mean Ms. Hamilton? The angel-hair lady?"

Intrigued, James cocked his head. "Angel-hair lady?"

"She has golden hair, like the angels," Dylan explained.

"Do you know her?"

"She came with the guy who took pictures of me and Dad. Only she didn't come here, just to the school."

"Did she now." It wasn't a question. But there were plenty of questions in James's eyes when he looked at Bryan. "Your dad didn't say anything about that."

Bryan's neck grew warm. "It was just a photo shoot. It probably took all of fifteen minutes. I don't think we said more than a dozen words to each other." He didn't mention the breakfast that followed. Or the impromptu, closed-door meeting they'd had in her office.

"Hmm. Well, young man, the Lord is waiting for us." James turned his attention to Dylan. "Let's head for the hills, as John Wayne used to say."

A puzzled expression flitted across Dylan's face. "Who's John Wayne?"

Shaking his head, James angled a look at Bryan. "If the younger generation doesn't even know who John Wayne is, then I'm overdue for retirement." James looked back at Dylan. "He starred in a lot of cowboy movies years ago."

"Oh." Dylan slid off the chair and turned to Bryan. "Do you want to come, Dad?"

It was hard to ignore the hopeful expression on his son's face, but he did his best, giving his standard response to this standard question. "Maybe next time." He kept hoping Dylan would get discouraged and stop asking, but so far he'd persisted.

"It would be nice if you came with Grandpa and me. It's a really pretty church, with stained-glass windows and a big steeple. And there's a big lawn in front that runs right down to the river."

"I remember, Dylan. I used to go there."

"How come you don't anymore?"

At a loss, Bryan gave his father a beseeching glance. The older man's eyes held their own silent entreaty, but he didn't repeat Dylan's question. Instead, he reached for his grandson's hand and led him to the door.

"Your dad's still trying to figure out the answer to that question himself. Now, I'll tell you what. After church, why don't we take a run over to Sugar Tree Park? Sure, and it's a lovely place on a summer evening, as I recall, and we can get ourselves an ice-cream cone at one of the stands by the lake. They have the best chocolate chip…."

As the door closed and his father's voice faded, Bryan took a deep breath. Telling his son that he was angry at God wasn't an option. That would only raise more questions that were even more difficult to answer. Maybe he ought to just go along with them in the future. It wouldn't kill him to sit in the church for an hour a week. Besides, he could use the quiet time. He didn't even have to listen if he chose not to. And his presence would get him off the hook with Dylan. Not to mention his father. Maybe that alone was a good enough reason to go.

"Look, Grandpa! It's the angel-hair lady!"

James followed the direction of Dylan's finger. He hadn't seen Amy Hamilton in a long time. As far as he knew, she had little cause to venture across the river to Hickory Mills. And his trips to the Davis Landing side of the Cumberland were rare. He'd never felt comfortable in the "uppity" section of town. The idea of stopping for ice cream at the park with Dylan had been a spur-of-the-moment suggestion to distract his grandson. But James wasn't sorry they'd come. He'd almost forgotten how lovely and peaceful the park was. The setting sun was turning the wayward drops of water from the spout in the middle of the lake to glistening diamonds. From their comfortable seat on a wooden bench, the spire of water was framed by a charming Victorian-styled gazebo on the other side of the lake, and the lush perennial beds surrounding the structure added a festive splash of color.

But he let his appreciative gaze wander over the scene for only a brief second before it swung back to the woman with the golden hair. It was Amy, all right. No question about it. She seemed to be lost in thought as she followed the path around the lake. He doubted whether she would even have noticed them in the fading light if Dylan hadn't greeted her as she drew close.

"Hi, Ms. Hamilton."

Startled, Amy jerked her head in the direction of the childish voice. She'd been so focused on sorting through her jumbled feelings about the situation with Bryan that she'd finally abandoned trying to catch up on some work in her condo. She'd hoped a brisk walk in the fresh air would clear her mind, but so far her foray into the September heat had only brought a flush to her face, one that deepened when she recognized Dylan. It took her a bit longer to realize that the older man beside him was James Healey. The last time she'd seen Bryan's father, six or seven years before, his hair had still been vibrant with color, his face smooth and unlined. It was clear that the death of his wife had taken a toll on him. But his smile was just as cordial as she remembered when he stood.

"Dylan spotted you first. It's good to see you, Amy."

She closed the distance between them and extended her hand. He took it between both of his, in a warm, caring clasp as she spoke. "Hello, Mr. Healey. Hi, Dylan."

"We're all adults now. Just call me James. Would you like to join us?"

When she hesitated, Dylan chimed in. "There's plenty of room." He scooted to the far side of the bench, leaving a wide gap in the middle. "You can have some of my ice cream," he added, as a further enticement.

"Now there's an offer that's hard to refuse."

She grinned and planted her hands on her hips. "But I'm selfish enough to want one all my own. Save that spot for me, okay?"

Before they could respond, she jogged off, returning a couple of minutes later with a large cone.

"Two scoops, I see," James teased.

"I'll pay for it tomorrow. It'll be diet yogurt for lunch."

"Doesn't look to me like you have to worry. You haven't changed a bit since high school."

"I hope that's not true." She gave him a look of mock horror, though she was more than half serious.

Catching her meaning, he gave a sage nod. "A very good point, indeed. I'm sure everyone changes inside as they age. At least I hope so. But on the outside, you look the same. You could still pass for a teenager. I'd have recognized you anywhere, even after all these years."

Because she couldn't respond in kind, she kept her reply innocuous. "It *has* been a long time."

"Too long. I was sorry to hear about your father. How is he doing?"

Her smile dimmed. "He's home now. Signs indicate that the transplant has been successful. But it's too soon to tell for sure. We're just taking it a day at a time. And trusting in God to give us the strength to see this through. I wish I had Mom's faith and fortitude. She's been a rock. Even with everything else that's happened, she just carries on."

"I did hear about Jeremy, and the changes at Hamilton Media."

"Hasn't everyone, thanks to the *Observer*." There was a bitter edge to her voice. "As if we needed that, on top of Dad's illness."

"Is your dad sick, Ms. Hamilton?"

She'd almost forgotten that Dylan was beside her. With an apologetic smile, she turned to him. "He was. But he's getting better now."

"I'd be sad if my dad got sick." He stopped eating his ice-cream cone and gave her a worried look.

Berating herself for discussing a subject that a child could find upsetting—especially a child who had lost his mother—Amy attempted to reassure him. "Well, I don't think that's going to happen. I've known your dad a long time. We went to school together. And he never got sick."

"You went to school with my dad?"

"Mmm-hmm. Right here in this town."

"Wow! Dad never told me that."

Why would he? What would be the point?

She was almost sorry now that she'd spilled the news. It might elicit questions that would be awkward for Bryan to answer.

"Well, it was a long time ago. Maybe he forgot. How's that ice cream?"

Instead of responding at once, Dylan took a big bite, leaving a white ring flecked with black around his mouth. "Great! Grandpa says this is the best ice cream in Tennessee."

"I think he's right."

As they talked, Amy made short work of her own treat, leaning over as it began to drip. After she popped the last bite of cone into her mouth, she wiped her hands on a paper napkin and stood. "Well, I've got to be off. I'll have to do a couple of extra laps around the lake to get rid of all those calories. But it was worth it."

James rose and extended his hand again. "It was good to see you, Amy. I'll keep your family in my prayers."

Blinking away a sudden stinging behind her eyes, Amy managed a smile. "Thank you. Bye, Dylan."

"Goodbye, Ms. Hamilton. I'll tell Dad we saw you."

Unsure how to respond, Amy merely lifted a hand and headed back down the path. She had no doubt that Dylan would follow through on his promise. And if he didn't, James would. But however he learned of her encounter with his family, Amy knew with absolute certainty that Bryan wouldn't be thrilled by the news.

"Staying late?"

Intent on her work, Amy finished typing the sentence before she looked up at Heather, who stood in her office doorway. "It's crunch time for the church newsletter. I haven't had a minute to work on it until this week, and it's scheduled to go to the printer in two days. Pastor Abernathy gave me one final addition after services last Sunday, or I'd have forgotten about it altogether."

"That's not like you. You never forget anything."

"Well, there's a first time for everything, I suppose."

Only since Bryan had reappeared, Heather reflected. But she kept that thought to herself. "I just wanted to let you know that we've got a layout done for Bryan's column. Ethan's photos turned out great. I'll run it by you tomorrow."

"Okay, thanks."

"Don't stay too late."

"Yeah, right."

As Heather departed, Amy refocused on the

newsletter. She still wasn't quite sure how Pastor Abernathy had convinced her to take it on after the former editor relocated to a different part of the state the year before. With his open manner, bright red hair, freckles and friendly face, the man could charm the cream from a cat. He'd been a great asset to Northside Community Church when their previous pastor retired four years before, breathing new life into the congregation. Within six months, he'd thrown the church's support behind a new sports program for at-risk youth, then started a meals-on-wheels program. Amy participated in that as well, delivering dinners one night a week in the outlying area.

In truth, though, she didn't mind. Her volunteer efforts for the church filled up the space in her life not occupied by work. And it was small repayment to the Lord for helping her find her way back to her faith.

Two hours later, Amy flexed the muscles in her back as she printed out the finished newsletter. Done for another month, except for the proofreading. She'd tackle that tomorrow, when she was fresher. Right now, her stomach was growling, reminding her that lunch was a distant memory.

As she swiveled toward her printer to

retrieve the pages, she heard the glass door that led from the elevator lobby into *Nashville Living* offices open, then whoosh shut. Odd. Few staffers ever stayed until—she checked her watch—almost eight o'clock.

She continued to listen, then froze when she heard a file drawer click shut. Apparently someone had just come in, not gone out. After all the trouble caused by Curtis Resnick, one of their accountants who had been fired six months before for embezzlement, Amy's antennae went up every time she saw or heard anything that seemed halfway suspicious. And a file drawer being closed this late in the evening, long after working hours, was more than a little suspicious.

Taking care to be as quiet as possible, Amy tiptoed to her door and peeked out. The place appeared to be deserted, the dim night-lights casting eerie shadows on the maze of cubicles that occupied the center of the second floor. Could she have imagined the noise? If so, she didn't want to embarrass herself by alerting security. Maybe she should take a quick look around first.

The newsletter printout still clutched in her hand, she moved cautiously through the offices, looking for signs of anything out of order. Nothing seemed abnormal, though, and as she completed her circuit she began to relax. Chalk it up to an overactive imagination, she chided herself. Next thing, she'd be hearing—

"I didn't know anyone else was here."

As the voice spoke behind her, Amy gasped and spun around, the papers in her hand flying in all directions. She stumbled back, losing her balance as the thin heel of her pump came down on an electrical safety strip. She would have fallen if a hand hadn't shot out to steady her. A hand that belonged to Bryan Healey.

"Sorry. I didn't mean to startle you."

Relief surged through her, and her muscles relaxed. But she couldn't stop the tremors that ran through her body like an aftershock. Nor could she seem to locate her voice.

"Amy?" Bryan stepped closer, reaching over to grasp her other arm as he scrutinized her face in the dim light. She looked shaken, and he could feel her trembling. "Are you okay?" His voice was now laced with concern.

With an effort, she gave a jerky nod. When she spoke, her voice was choppy. "We had some…problems…with an employee…a few months ago. I still get spooked by…by noises at night, when I'm here alone."

Bryan figured she was here alone at night a lot, since she'd always placed such a high priority on her career. Long hours would be part of her routine. But being accosted in the darkened offices wouldn't be. Contrition flooded his face. "I'm sorry. Look, do you want to sit down for a minute?"

Shaking her head, she reached up to brush her hair back from her face, and he let his hands drop to his sides. Even in the dim light, he could see that her fingers were still unsteady.

"What are you doing here?" she asked.

"I had to leave early to attend a program this afternoon at Dylan's school. I came back to make up the time after I went home for dinner."

"That's not necessary, Bryan. We understand when people have family commitments."

Shrugging, he bent down and began gathering up the papers she'd dropped. "I don't want to shortchange my job."

She joined him on the floor, reaching for a sheet that had wedged itself under a printer stand. "I'm not worried about that."

When he didn't respond, she gave him a quick glance. He was staring at the cover page for the newsletter, and there was a puzzled look on his face.

Amy rose, and he followed, handing over

the sheets of paper he'd gathered as she answered his unasked question. "It's the church newsletter."

"I figured that. Why do you have it?"

"I'm the editor."

He gave her a blank look. "What?"

"I'm the editor."

Bryan tried to digest that information. Though Amy's church attendance had been regular in high school—Wallace wouldn't have allowed otherwise—he knew she'd fallen away from her faith in college, treating it as excess baggage. He'd seen how she lived, when he'd made that unannounced visit during her freshman year. She'd taken him to a wild frat party, where excessive drinking seemed to be the main activity. Despite her urging, he'd declined to participate. But that hadn't stopped her. She'd called him a stick-in-the-mud, then proceeded to down several drinks. When she became tipsy, Bryan had taken her back to her apartment, only to discover that she shared it with two other girls, including one who'd had a live-in boyfriend.

Shock had been too mild a word to describe Bryan's reaction to her lifestyle. Although he'd gone east hoping to convince her to re-consider her demand for space and to give their relationship another try, he'd returned home with a different mind-set. While part of him was still in love with the girl he'd idolized throughout high school, he'd been turned off by the way she lived, unable to reconcile it to his values. In his heart, he'd known then that Amy wasn't for him. She had strayed too far from the principles and the faith that were the cornerstone of his life.

Yet now it seemed she'd found her way back to faith, even as his own had wavered. The irony wasn't lost on him.

As Amy watched Bryan process her response and come to the obvious conclusion, she wasn't surprised at his astonishment. She knew what he'd thought about her lifestyle in college. Or rather, what he had perceived her lifestyle to be after that awful, unannounced visit he'd made. While it was true that she'd strayed from her faith, most of the other conclusions he'd come to during that visit had been wrong. Yes, she'd had too much to drink at that party. But that was the first—and only—time she'd done that. She hadn't liked alcohol back then. She still didn't. She wasn't even sure what had prompted her uncharacteristic actions that night. Immaturity, most likely. And as for her living arrangements…she hadn't approved of Sheila's live-in boyfriend, either. He'd only appeared on the scene that week, and a few days later, the two of them had moved out. Of course, Bryan didn't know any of that. Nor had she tried to clarify the situation. In those days, she'd still wanted space. She'd figured they could straighten the mess out someday. But she'd figured wrong.

"Does that mean you're attending church again?" His voice was cautious, as if he still couldn't quite believe it.

"Yes."

Bryan was tempted to ask how she'd found her way back to God. But that wasn't an appropriate question. The topic was too personal. And their relationship was strictly business.

Shoving his hands in his pockets, he took a step back. "Well, I need to get to work. I don't want to be here until midnight."

She'd already told him he didn't need to make up the time. She wasn't going to repeat it. If he wanted to stay, that was his decision. "And I need to go home and have some dinner. I'll see you tomorrow."

Without waiting for a response, Amy edged past him and headed back to her office to retrieve her purse. She wasted no time leaving, slipping out the door as quietly as she could, not willing to risk another encounter with Bryan tonight. Yet the one she'd just had wasn't easy to dismiss. Even as she rode down in the elevator minutes later, she could still feel the touch of his strong hands on her arms, could see the concern on his face as he'd stared at her in the shadowy light. For the first time since his return, he'd looked at her with caring. Prompted, she knew, by simple human consideration. But the effect had been devastating, nonetheless, bringing back memories of other times he'd touched her, other times he'd looked at her with the deep green eyes that had once been soft with tenderness.

She was still trembling when she stepped off the elevator. She wanted to attribute her reaction to the shock of being startled in the deserted office, to fear that an intruder had trespassed onto family property. But she knew better. She trembled now from fear of another kind, sparked by the knowledge that an intruder had, indeed, trespassed tonight. Onto her heart. And that he'd taken something of great value, something she desperately needed for peace of mind. For survival, even.

Her last shred of illusion that Bryan Healey was history.

Chapter Five

"Is this Amy Hamilton?"

The childish voice on the other end of the phone line brought a puzzled expression to Amy's face. "Yes. Who's calling?"

"This is Dylan Healey."

Her puzzlement deepened. Why would Bryan's son be calling her? Especially at home? "Hello, Dylan." She consulted her watch. Nine o'clock. Shouldn't he be in bed by now? "Is everything all right?"

"Yeah. I just wanted to invite you to a party."

"A party?"

"Uh-huh. My grandpa's retiring. That means he won't have to go to work anymore. Anyway, they're having a party for him. Since I won't know hardly anybody there, I thought maybe you might want to come."

Amy didn't even have to ask to know that Bryan had no clue his son had placed this call. As she tried to figure out how to respond, she heard a muffled voice in the background, then the muted sound of Dylan responding. An exchange took place, and even though the words were indistinct, she could hear her name. The next thing she knew, Bryan was on the phone.

"Amy?" His tone was tentative.

"Yes."

A sigh of frustration—or disgust—came over the line. Amy couldn't tell which. "Sorry about this. I had no idea Dylan was going to call you."

"It's okay. A bit unexpected, though. How in the world did he get my number?"

"That's what I just ferreted out. It seems he asked Dad to show him your name in the church directory. He remembered the page number and looked it up a little while ago."

"Resourceful little guy."

"That's one way to describe him. Anyway, sorry we bothered you."

"Not a problem. I didn't realize your dad was retiring."

"Yeah. Friday's his last day."

"Give him my best wishes, would you? I'd have told him myself if I'd known about it when I saw him." As soon as she said the words, Amy regretted them. What if, by chance, James or Dylan hadn't told Bryan about the encounter in the park? But his next comment confirmed that they had.

"Dad mentioned that he and Dylan ran into you Sunday evening."

"Yes. I don't know who was more surprised, me or them. I haven't seen your dad in years. He looked good."

"He's aged quite a bit."

"Haven't we all."

"Not to hear Dad talk. He was amazed at how little you've changed."

"Your dad always did have a bit of the blarney in his soul."

"Not this time."

Was that a backhanded compliment? Amy wondered in surprise. Then she answered her own question. No, of course not. Bryan was the last man on earth who would say anything nice about her. No doubt he'd meant it as a simple statement of fact. In truth, she didn't look a whole lot different on the outside. Inside…that was another story. Bryan might be surprised if he could see into her heart. "Well, you know what they say. Never judge a book by its cover." She tried for a flippant tone but didn't quite pull it off.

The sound of a childish voice in the background came over the line, and once more Amy heard a muffled exchange before Bryan spoke to her again. "Sorry. My son is nothing if not persistent. The party has been the hot topic of conversation all week."

"It's a nice tribute for your dad."

Before he could respond, another voice joined in the conversation from his end. An older voice. Bryan must have covered the mouthpiece, because Amy could only pick up a phrase or two. Including something that sounded like, "busy lady" and "have time for parties like this."

When he came back on the line, she heard the edge of irritation in his voice. "Sorry again. They're ganging up on me over here. I'd better get off the phone before they wrestle it away from me."

"Does your dad want me to come, too?"

There was a slight hesitation before he gave a cautious response. "He said you'd be welcome, but I told them both that you wouldn't have—"

"I'd like to come, actually."

Dead silence greeted her comment. Bryan seemed as shocked by her words as she was. And she had no idea where they'd come from.

The last thing she ought to do was involve herself with Bryan's family. He'd been clear about the fact that he didn't want any more contact with her than necessary. So why on earth had she put him in such an awkward position? It made no sense.

Backtracking quickly, Amy spoke again. "Of course, I realize this is more for friends and family. Just give your dad my best, and tell Dylan I'm sure I'll see him again soon. Maybe even at the park."

"Listen, Amy—"

"Look, it's okay. I have to run now. I'll see you at the office." Without waiting for a reply, she set the phone back in the cradle.

Rattled, Amy sank onto one of the stools at the small island in her kitchen. Talk about a dumb move. Not to mention embarrassing. A flush rose on her cheeks, and she closed her eyes, wishing she could relive the past few minutes. She should have laughed off the call and gotten off the phone as fast as she could. Instead, the conversation had strayed to more personal topics. Then she'd practically invited herself to the party, even though she'd been on no one's original guest list—except Dylan's. What must Bryan think?

Nothing good, she was sure. The best she could hope for was that he would forget about the whole thing.

"Got a minute?"

At the sound of Bryan's voice Amy raised her head, the page proofs in front of her instantly forgotten. "Sure."

He took two steps into her office, then stuck his hands in the pockets of his khaki slacks. "Dad wanted me try asking again about the party. He'd like you to come. Dylan would, too."

But I don't. He didn't have to say the words for the message to come across loud and clear. Amy swallowed past her hurt and pasted on a smile. "Thanks. I appreciate the thought. But I'll pass."

Relief coursed through Bryan, though he tried to keep his face impassive. He'd promised to ask her again, and he had. Now he could walk out the door and forget about it.

Except something in Amy's eyes tugged at his conscience. Something that looked a lot like hurt. He supposed he hadn't issued the invitation with a whole lot of enthusiasm. But what did she expect? It hadn't been his idea in the first place. If his father and Dylan hadn't pestered him so much, he'd have let it drop last night. In fact, if he'd had any sense, he would have. For some reason, he had a feeling that by bringing it up again, he'd made things worse. And that bothered him. More than it should. Enough that he figured he'd better try again. He may not like Amy Hamilton, but that was no excuse to be unkind.

"Look, it would mean a lot to Dad. I know he always enjoyed your company, and running into you in the park must have reminded him of…well, it brought back memories for him."

Although Amy was sorry now she'd ever shown an interest in attending the party, she liked James Healey. His delight at seeing her in the park had seemed genuine, and he'd always been kind to her when she and Bryan were dating. She hated to decline if the older man was sincere in his invitation. But it would be awkward. Maybe she could just show up for a few minutes, offer her best wishes and make a quick exit. That might be manageable.

"When is it again?" she stalled.

"Saturday from five to eight, at The Smokehouse." The popular eatery was halfway between Davis Landing and Nashville, an easy fifteen-minute drive. "It will just be snacks and beverages and a cake, more like an open house where people can come and go whenever they like."

That was even better. She could handle that. "All right. I'll stop by for a few minutes."

"Great. I'll let Dad—and Dylan—know."

As Bryan left Amy's office and headed back toward his cubicle, he had mixed emotions about the outcome of their conversation. On one hand, he was glad she'd agreed to go, for Dad's and Dylan's sake. On the other hand, her presence wasn't going to add to his enjoyment of the party one iota. But the party wasn't about him, he reminded himself. It was his dad's night. And if James wanted Amy there, Bryan would just have to live with it. He'd be polite, of course. Engage in a few words of small talk. And then he'd do his best to ignore her.

Because they had nothing to say to each other.

Amy reached for a carrot stick, swirled it in the dip and turned to survey the banquet room at The Smokehouse. She hadn't been to the restaurant in a long time, but little had changed. The rustic Appalachian decor, with hooked rugs on the pine floor and quilts on the walls, was the same as she remembered from years ago. The only thing unfamiliar in the room was the people.

From the turnout, though, it was clear that James Healey had been well-liked at work. He was still standing near the door, and a steady stream of colleagues and co-workers had greeted him in the ten minutes since she'd arrived. And she was glad she'd come. His warmth when he'd gripped her hand in welcome had been sincere. That alone had made the trip worthwhile. But he was the only one who had talked to her. Bryan and Dylan were nowhere to be seen. She'd spotted Bryan's brother, Kevin, across the room, and he'd raised a hand in greeting when he saw her. But his attention had quickly been diverted by a man and woman beside him. Trying not to look obvious, Amy checked her watch. After a trip to the ladies' room, she could make a discreet exit. No one would miss her, anyway.

By the time she reentered the room, the crowd had thickened. With a murmured "excuse me," she juggled her cup of soda and eased by two men who looked close to James's age, wedging herself against the wall between them and a large potted palm. The exit was across the room, and she didn't relish wading through the sea of people. But there was no other way out.

Just as she was about to take the plunge, a conversation on the other side of the palm caught her attention. She'd recognize Bryan's voice anywhere. And she was pretty sure he was talking to Kevin.

"…glad to be home?"

"Yeah. I would have liked to come back years ago." That was Bryan.

"You could have."

"I had obligations."

"They weren't your obligations. She wasn't your mother."

"No. But she was Darlene's. She didn't want to leave her home, and she couldn't manage it on her own anymore. There wasn't anyone else to help."

"Bryan, you cut her grass, took care of her house, shuttled her to the doctor…that was above and beyond. Especially with everything else you were trying to cope with."

"It was the right thing to do, for a lot of reasons. She was devastated when Darlene died." There was a slight lapse in the conversation, and Amy heard the clink of ice in a glass, as if someone had just taken a long gulp. When Bryan continued, his voice was subdued. "I guess, in some way, I was trying to make amends. To apologize. I knew we were pushing our luck by waiting. The doctors warned us how dangerous it could be. But Darlene was determined to reach thirty weeks…" Bryan's voice roughened, and he cleared his throat. "I should have insisted that we follow the doctor's advice."

"You did what you thought was right at the time, Bryan. It doesn't do any good to keep beating yourself up over it. If you'd taken action sooner, you might have lost Dylan. Or both of them."

"Yeah." The heaviness in Bryan's voice tore at Amy's heart. When she'd read the information on the Net about preeclampsia, she'd suspected Bryan might have faced the very dilemma he and Kevin were discussing. Now her suspicion was confirmed. What a terrible choice he'd faced. Save your wife, lose your son. Save your son, lose your wife. Or, as Kevin had said, lose both. How did a man cope with that kind of dilemma—and with the consequences?

"…kind of weird to work for someone you once considered marrying."

Amy had missed a few lines of conversation, but now her ears perked back up at Kevin's comment.

"I don't see that much of her."

"She's still gorgeous."

"Yeah. She's still the same in a lot of ways." There was a touch of bitter irony in Bryan's voice.

"I'm picking up that that's not a good thing. Must have something to do with the reason you two broke up. You always were pretty closemouthed about that."

"We just went different directions."

"Well, you might have taken different routes, but you both ended up back home. Seems a little like fate to me."

Amy was growing more uncomfortable by the second. But now she was trapped. If she stepped out, they'd realize she'd been eavesdropping on a very private conversation. Maybe she should just lay low until they moved somewhere else in the room. She was pretty hidden, and….

Suddenly one of the men she'd squeezed past threw out his arm to emphasize a point, knocking the soda cup from her hand. The dark liquid splashed against her white camisole top, and she stared in dismay as a huge, irregular splotch formed right in the middle of the snowy expanse, then slowly spread outward.

The commotion drew the attention of guests in the immediate vicinity—including Dylan, who emerged from the forest of legs just in time to witness the whole thing.

"Hi, Ms. Hamilton." He bounded over, observing her with interest through the lenses of his horn-rimmed glasses, his youthful high-pitched voice rising above the din of conversation in the room. "You spilled your drink. I do that sometimes, too."

"Oh, my, I'm so sorry, pretty lady." The older man turned to her, his face contrite.

As Amy dabbed at the stain to no effect, she saw in her peripheral vision that Bryan and his brother had emerged from the other side of the palm. Her hair had swung forward, covering much of her face, but she doubted the warm rush of color in her cheeks would subside before she was forced to look over at them.

"Let me get some paper napkins," Kevin said.

Raising her head, Amy spoke. "Don't worry about it. I was just leaving anyway."

"I don't think paper napkins are going to help much," Bryan noted.

Turning to him, Amy saw that his attention

was focused on the stain. Which only fanned the flame in her cheeks. As she looked back toward Kevin, she noticed his gaze was fixed on her cheeks. That wasn't much better. Kevin's perceptive eyes reflected his years of training as a trial lawyer, and she had the feeling he was seeing far more than she intended to reveal.

Dylan's face fell. "Do you have to go already?"

Before she could respond, Bryan stepped in. "Dylan, go help Uncle Kevin get some napkins."

"But he—"

"Now."

With a grumble, the boy moved off with Kevin. The two older men also edged away, leaving Amy and Bryan sequestered beside the palm. From his speculative expression, it was clear that he was wondering just how much of his conversation she had overheard. Forcing her lips into a bright smile, she decided that escape was her best option. "Look, I think I'll just head out. Tell your dad goodbye for me, would you?"

When she started to move away, Bryan fell into step beside her. "I'll walk you to your car."

"That's not necessary."

"Dad would be disappointed if I let a lady leave a party unescorted."

After a slight hesitation, she capitulated with a shrug. "Well, we can't have that."

She resumed her trek to the door, impressed by Bryan's manners. Even as a teenager, they'd been flawless. A true Southern gentleman, in the best sense of the word. Kind and considerate even to people he disliked. Like her.

They passed Kevin and Dylan on the way out. "I'll be back in a minute, after I see Amy to her car. Dylan, stay with Uncle Kevin."

The disappointed look on Dylan's face tugged at her heart. She leaned down to his level, resisting a temptation to brush his unruly hair back from his face. Instead, she placed a hand on his shoulder. "Thank you for inviting me tonight. Maybe one of these Sundays we can have another ice-cream party in the park with your grandpa."

His face brightened. "That would be fun. Dad might even come the next time." Then his expression grew troubled. "Except Dad doesn't go to church anymore."

Jolted, Amy stared at Dylan. Bryan's faith had always been strong and sure. Then again, he'd been through a lot these past few years. She supposed the tragedy that had darkened his life could easily have dimmed his faith, as well. Before she had time to digest Dylan's bombshell, Bryan's hand on her elbow urged her back up.

"There's a break in the crowd. This is a good time to work our way through." His voice was conversational, but the tense line of his jaw told Amy that he wasn't happy about the airing of his lapsed faith. He remained silent until they stepped outside. "Where are you parked?"

"Right over there." She gestured to her left. "Thanks for walking me out, but I can take it from here."

Puzzled, Bryan scanned the section of the lot she'd pointed to. He didn't see any high-end cars even close to the area Amy had indicated. Just serviceable vehicles, the kind regular people drove. Nothing like the sporty red convertible Wallace had given her for her sixteenth birthday, which had been the envy of every kid at high school. "Which one is yours?"

"The dark blue one." She started toward it, digging for her keys in her purse. To her surprise, he again fell in step beside her.

When she stopped beside a Toyota Camry, he was more bewildered than ever. "This is your car?"

"Yes." She withdrew her keys and looked up at him. "Why?" But she already had her answer. His face spoke volumes. All her life, she'd lived the good life: grown up in the finest house in Davis Landing, worn designer clothes, traveled all over the world for vacations and holidays. It was a life few experienced, and one she'd taken for granted—expected, even—during her growing-up years. Over time, she'd learned to appreciate the privileges she'd enjoyed, but even more importantly, she'd learned she didn't need them. The trappings of wealth were nice, but they didn't bring happiness. That had to come from inside, from a solid faith and a recognition that the most important things in life aren't things at all.

Before Bryan could answer, she spoke again, a wistful smile just touching the corners of her mouth. "I gave up red sports cars a long time ago."

And a lot of other things, too. She didn't say those words, but Bryan heard the implication. A few minutes earlier, he'd told Kevin that Amy hadn't changed. Now he wondered. There was something in her eyes—a mellowness, a maturity, a quiet acceptance of the hand life had dealt her—that hadn't been there before. Or had his memories of her from the past been so vivid they'd blinded him to the present?

With that unexpected and disconcerting thought came a reaction that was even more disturbing. As the golden light of late afternoon gilded her hair, as he recalled its silken feel against his fingers from many years before, he suddenly wanted to reach out and lift a few strands, weigh them in his hand, test whether that, at least, had remained unchanged.

Shaken by the urge, he jammed his hands in his pockets. When he spoke, his tone was more curt than he intended. "Drive safe."

Ignoring the surprised expression on her face, he turned and strode away without a backward look.

Kevin crossed his ankle over his knee, folded his hands across his stomach and leaned back in the rocking chair. James had offered to put Dylan to bed, and the two brothers had moved out to the back porch, where they'd often spent late-summer evenings just like this drinking lemonade and swatting at mosquitoes as they tried to catch a breeze off the river. "Seems like old times, doesn't it?"

"Yeah." Bryan stretched his legs out in

front of him and stared at the stars twinkling in the night sky.

"I think Dad had a good time tonight. It was a nice party."

"Yeah."

"I was surprised to see Amy there." When that comment elicited no reply, he continued. "Dad was glad she came. He always did like her."

"Yeah."

Bryan's one-word responses didn't seem to satisfy Kevin. His brother stopped rocking and leaned forward, clasping his hands between his knees. "So what gives with you two?"

Frowning, Bryan transferred his attention from the stars to his brother. "What do you mean?"

"You come home and go to work for your old girlfriend. Next thing I know, she's at Dad's party. Dylan is enamored with her. The evidence suggests that there's more here than an employer/employee relationship."

James Healey had always been the diplomat in the family. Their mother had been more direct, a trait she'd passed on to both her sons—one Bryan now wished had bypassed his brother. They were moving onto shaky ground, and he didn't want to go there. Not after this afternoon in the parking lot. He'd been distracted ever since, clueless about the reason for his odd reaction. And he didn't want it dissected by one of Houston's hottest young prosecuting attorneys. "You know better than to come to conclusions based on circumstantial evidence."

"That's not all I'm basing them on."

"Stop being an attorney, Kevin."

"Okay. I'll just be a brother."

Stifling a sigh, Bryan raked his fingers through his hair. That might be worse. "Just let it go, okay?"

Kevin ignored him. "I thought you told me years ago that you and Amy were history."

"We are."

"That's not what it looked like tonight."

The twin furrows between Bryan's eyebrows deepened. "What are you talking about?"

"Did you look at Amy?"

"Of course I looked at her. She was only standing two feet away."

"Did you look into her eyes?"

"Where is this line of questioning leading, Counselor?"

"Okay, I'll cut to the chase. It's my considered opinion that, without a whole lot of encouragement, Amy Hamilton would be very willing to pick up where you guys left off."

Bryan stared at him. "You're nuts."

"Am I?"

"Yeah, you are. She didn't want anything to do with me years ago. Why would she change her mind now?"

Two beats of silence passed. "Then she's the one who broke things off?"

A flush rose on the back of Bryan's neck. He hadn't shared the details of the breakup with his family back then. And he hadn't planned to start now. But he'd walked right into Kevin's trap, revealing far more than he'd intended. He'd sure hate to be on a witness stand if his brother was doing the interrogation. "More or less," he conceded, with reluctance. "She said she wanted space, that she needed time. I wanted a family, and the sooner the better. Plus, her lifestyle in college wasn't…it didn't mesh with my values."

Once more, Kevin leaned back and started rocking, his face thoughtful. "Maybe she just wasn't ready to make a commitment. Women don't like to be rushed. And consider her upbringing—the oldest daughter in the very visible Hamilton dynasty. I suspect Wallace can be very demanding. Maybe she needed a break from family obligations before she committed to starting a family of her own. As for her lifestyle in college—lots of people do things when they leave home for the first time that they later regret."

Regret. That was something else he'd seen in Amy's eyes today in the parking lot at the restaurant. He hadn't recognized it then; now it became clear. But regret about what? And could Kevin be right? Had he pushed too hard when he and Amy were in college? He knew Amy loved her father, but Wallace Hamilton was a force to be reckoned with. Amy had told him herself that the family patriarch could be a hard taskmaster. Maybe she *had* needed a break from family demands and obligations, a chance to experience life on her terms, before settling down to the obligations that creating her own family would entail.

"Anyway, if you ask me, Amy still has feelings for you."

Still stunned by his new insight, it took a second for Kevin's conjecture to sink in. That, too, jolted him. But before he could respond, James stepped through the screen door.

"It took a while to get him settled. He was still too excited from the party to sit still, let alone lie down. But I told him some stories about the two of you growing up, and that put him to sleep in no time."

Chuckling, Kevin rose. "We were that boring, huh?"

"You were good boys."

"Boring," Kevin reasserted with a grin. "I'm heading to bed, Dad. After I call Karen and say good-night to Megan and Daniel, of course."

"Give them all my love. And tell them I'm sorry again they missed the party. But I'm sure Karen would rather be here than coping with two raging cases of poison ivy."

"You can say that again. Too bad I had to miss all that fun." An unrepentant grin flashed across Kevin's face. "Anyway, I'll pass on your message. Good night, Bryan."

As the screen door closed behind Kevin, James claimed his seat in the rocking chair. "It was a fine party. It warmed my heart that so many people came. Even Amy stopped by. Such a nice girl. I'm surprised she isn't married by now."

A few weeks ago, Bryan would have responded as he'd done directly to her at his welcome lunch at the office. That she'd always had more important things to do. Since he wasn't as confident in that explanation now, he remained silent.

"Speaking of marriage, have you ever given any thought to another walk down the aisle, Bryan?"

No question about it, this was a night for surprises. Bryan stared at his father. "You think I should get married again?"

The rhythmic creak of the rocking chair was steady in the still night. "It might be something to consider. You're still a young man. And Dylan, sure now, he could use a mother. The way he's taken to Amy…well, it's a sign that he's looking for a woman's touch in his life."

Amy as a mother figure? It was hard to imagine. Though not as hard as it might have been a few weeks before, Bryan admitted, as he turned to stare out into the dark night, into the shadows where the dim porch light didn't reach. The little boy did seem drawn to her, and there had been a tender warmth in Amy's eyes whenever she'd spoken to his son. Still, the notion that he'd consider renewing their relationship was absurd. They had too much baggage, for one thing. Besides, he'd taken a chance on love twice and lost both times. He couldn't risk that kind of loss again.

Nor could he dishonor the memory of Darlene by going back to his first love. Wouldn't that somehow denigrate what they'd had? Suggest that he'd settled for second best when his first love had rejected him? In fact, that wasn't the case at all. He'd loved Darlene with his whole heart. In a different way than he'd loved Amy, but with just as much loyalty and conviction. He would never want anyone to think otherwise.

Yet there were times in the past couple of years when he'd longed for someone to fill the empty place in his heart left by Darlene's death. Her passing had created a void in his life, an emptiness so crushing that it sometimes took his breath away and made him yearn for the warmth of a deep and satisfying love, for the companionship and comfort offered by a strong marriage. He was human, after all. And as his father had said, he was still a young man.

Redirecting his attention to James, Bryan saw that the older man was watching him with eyes that were warm and wise, as if he could see right into his heart and understood his dilemma. His next words seemed to confirm that.

"I know you loved Darlene, Bryan. She was a fine woman. And she gave you a fine son.

But she's gone now. And I don't think she—or the Lord—would want you to walk through the rest of your life alone. It would be wrong to waste all the love you have in your heart. You're the kind of man who should be sharing that love with a family of his own."

"I have Dylan."

"That you do. But you have a great capacity for love, son. There's plenty more in your heart to spread around."

It was difficult to speak past the lump in his throat. "There's a risk in loving."

"That there is. Though it seems worth the taking to me."

"I'm not sure about that."

"You've had some hard days, Bryan, true enough. But think of all the good days, too. Days you wouldn't have known if you hadn't opened your heart to love."

There was no arguing with that. Bryan's happiest times had all come about because of love. Love for his family, love for Amy, love for Darlene, love for Dylan. Yet even if his father was right, even if he found the courage to pursue another romance, to risk rejection and loss again, it wouldn't be with Amy. It couldn't be. Maybe he'd pushed too hard when they were younger. Maybe she'd changed in the years since they'd parted. Maybe, if they were meeting now for the first time, something might spark between them. But as it was, there was just too much water under the bridge, too much history between them.

His father was right about something else, too. Dylan did need a mother. Perhaps he ought to consider remarriage for that reason alone. But his heart just wasn't in it. "You make some good points, Dad. But I wouldn't even know where to start."

"Close to home isn't a bad place. Some people wander all over the world looking for answers, only to discover that they were right in their own backyard all along."

"Are you talking about Amy?"

The older man lifted one shoulder. "She's a nice girl."

"What we had died a long time ago, Dad."

The older man digested that for a moment. "You know, back in Ireland, we didn't have fancy things like central heat when I was a boy, growing up on the farm. Just a big fireplace. When I was old enough, it was my job to get the peat fire going in the morning. Sure, I'll always remember those chilly winter dawns, when the grate would look black and cold. But after I stirred up the ashes a wee bit, I almost always found some embers still glowing. And with a little coaxing, they'd spark back to life. Before long I'd have a nice, warm fire going to chase away the chill of the morn."

Stories of James's boyhood had been standard fare when Bryan was growing up, and often they had a point. Like this one. A point Kevin had made by taking a more direct approach, saying that he thought Amy would be willing to pick up where they'd left off, and that she still had feelings for him. It seemed James had come to the same conclusion. But Bryan wasn't nearly as sure.

"You may be jumping to conclusions about Amy," he cautioned his father. "Our romance happened a long time ago. I'm not sure there are any embers left in her heart to be stirred, even if I was so inclined."

Instead of responding at once, the older man rose and stretched. "I think I'll call it a night myself." He turned toward the house, pausing after he pulled open the screen door to cast one parting comment over his shoulder. "And by the way, I wasn't talking about Amy."

Chapter Six

The jarring ring of the bedside phone brought Amy instantly awake, and she squinted at the digital face of the clock on her nightstand. A few minutes past midnight. Not good. A surge of adrenaline rushed through her, making every nerve ending tingle, and her pulse tripped into double time as she groped for the handset and struggled to a sitting position. Ever since Wallace had become ill, she'd dreaded late-night calls.

"Hello?"

"Amy, it's Melissa."

If Amy hadn't already been sitting, she would have ended up in a heap on the floor. Relief that there was no emergency with her father, coupled with shock that her runaway sister was calling, had rendered her legs useless.

"Melissa? Where are you? Do you have any idea how worried everyone's been?"

When the only response to her critical, interrogatory tone was a sniffle, followed by a choked sob, Amy forced herself to take a deep breath. *Calm down. If you upset her too much, she'll hang up. And we'll be no closer to knowing her whereabouts.* She tried again, gentling her voice. "Melissa, hey, it's okay. I'm sorry. With everything that's been going on, I got a little spooked by the late call. Are you okay?"

The sniffles increased. Instead of answering Amy's question, she asked one of her own. "How's Dad?"

"He had the transplant, and he's home now. But he's still under close supervision."

"When you said a lot's been going on, I—I thought maybe Dad was worse."

How much should she reveal about the family's problems? Amy wondered. She didn't want to keep her sister in the dark, but from Melissa's tearful voice, it sounded as if she had troubles of her own. Still, her sister had a right to know at least the basics. "There have been a few other surprises. On the good side, Heather and Ethan got engaged. On the not-so-good side, we found out that Jeremy isn't Dad's biological son. A fact that the

Observer was kind enough to broadcast to the world. Jeremy's left town to find his father's family, and Tim is running Hamilton Media."

"Wow."

That single, faintly uttered word about summed up life in the Hamilton family for the past few months, Amy acknowledged, her lips twisting into a humorless smile. "Yeah. Wow."

"Look…the family has enough to worry about already. This probably isn't a good time to…to talk about me. I'll just call another—"

"Melissa, we're already worried about you," Amy interrupted. "Dad asks about you all the time. When are you coming home?"

"I—I'm not sure."

"At least tell me where you are."

"I'm in Detroit. With Dean."

Amy already knew about Melissa's traveling companion. It paid to have a police officer for a brother—the blue sheep of the family, as they affectionately called Chris, since he was the only sibling to stray from the Hamilton Media fold. He'd done some quiet checking and discovered that Dean Orton, Melissa's boyfriend, had left town with no forwarding address at the same time she had disappeared. This wasn't the first time that Melissa had run away from problems instead of facing them. That's why the family hadn't panicked—especially after Chris had turned up the information on Dean. Amy supposed some might find the long-haired, cowboy-boot-clad rock musician attractive, but he'd always struck her as a user. Too bad Melissa hadn't shared that assessment. If she had, this whole mess could have been avoided.

"We know you're with Dean, Melissa. Chris did some unofficial investigating. Look, if money's an issue, I'll send you enough for a plane ticket. Or I'll even come and get you if you want."

"I—I can't come home, Amy." Melissa's voice was small—and scared.

"Of course you can, honey. Dad and Mom will welcome you back with open arms. You know that."

"Not when they know about the…baby."

As Melissa whispered the last word, Amy's stomach clenched into a tight knot. *Please, God, not that! How much can one family take before it starts to crumble?* For a fleeting second, Amy was tempted to hang up the phone, to pretend that this call had never happened, that the youngest Hamilton was just off "finding herself" again, that she'd reappear just as suddenly as she'd disappeared and everything would return to normal. But a baby—that changed everything. Forever. Unless maybe—*please, Lord, let it be so*—she had come to the wrong conclusion.

The silence on the other end of the line— almost as if Melissa was holding her breath— was ominous, yet Amy forced herself to ask the question. "Are you telling me that you're pregnant, Lissa?"

It had been years since Amy had used that affectionate childhood nickname for her sister, one she'd coined and reserved for occasions when the two of them had a heart-to-heart talk. That hadn't happened often; most of the time Melissa had been too busy trying to compete with her popular, successful older sister. But now, calling up that endearment from the past had been the right thing to do. Amy's gentle, sympathetic tone unleashed a torrent of tears on the other end of the phone, along with a rush of words she couldn't begin to decipher.

Several minutes passed before Melissa could regain enough control to sound coherent. Then, at Amy's request, she took a deep breath and started over. Even so, her words were choppy, and her voice was laced with panic. "I know what I did was…was wrong. But I felt so alone when…when Dad got sick. And s-scared. Dean said he'd take care of me, and that we'd get married. But now h-he's having second thoughts. And he's not happy about the baby. I want to come home, Amy, but I—I'm too ashamed. I can't bring another scandal down on the family."

"Melissa, we love you. The Hamiltons are strong. We can handle this." Amy managed a firm, reassuring tone despite the uncertainty that fluttered in her stomach.

"Dad and Mom will be s-so disappointed in me."

Amy didn't dispute that. Wallace and Nora had raised their children with sound values, and had instilled in them a clear understanding of right and wrong. Yet they also believed in a key tenet of their faith—forgiveness. Too bad the strength of that conviction had to be tested now, in the midst of all the other crises they faced.

"They still love you, Melissa. We all do. Please, come home. You need medical care. You shouldn't be traipsing all over the country following some rock band around."

"I—I can't. Not yet, anyway. I just needed to hear a…a friendly voice. I feel so alone and so scared. I don't know how to be a mother, and I'm not sure I even love Dean anymore.

But I have to work this out myself. I've always relied on the family to clean up my messes, to come to my rescue. It's time I took responsibility for my own actions. I need to deal with this problem on my own."

Amy wasn't sure she liked the sound of that. A pregnancy wasn't a problem; it was a child. "Is Dean pushing you to…do something about the baby?"

There was a second of shocked silence. Much to Amy's relief, Melissa's voice was strong—and sure—when she responded. "If you mean, did he suggest an abortion, the answer is yes. But I told him that's out of the question. Why should an innocent child suffer because we made a mistake? I'm having the baby. I know where my child belongs. With me. I just need to figure out where *I* belong."

The conviction in Melissa's voice impressed Amy. Her baby sister seemed to be growing up, after all. Though she'd chosen the hard way, that was for sure. As for where she belonged—Amy knew beyond the shadow of a doubt that it wasn't with Dean. "You belong here, with us," she told Melissa.

"Maybe. But I need to work that out for myself. Listen, Amy, would it be okay if I call you again, just to talk? With Heather still living at home, I'm afraid Mom might answer the phone if I call there, and I don't want to talk to her yet."

"Of course. Anytime. I mean that, Lissa."

The tears were back in Melissa's voice. "I know. Thank you, Amy."

"That's what family's for."

"I'm beginning to realize that."

"Can I at least tell the family you called? They've all been worried sick about you."

"Yeah…I guess so. And give them my love. But don't tell them about the baby, okay?" When Amy hesitated, Melissa pressed the issue. "Please, Amy. Promise me you'll keep my secret."

It was hard to ignore the pleading note in Melissa's voice. Against her better judgment, Amy agreed. "All right. If you promise me you'll keep in touch."

"I will. I'll call again as soon as I've decided what to do. Thanks, Amy."

"No thanks needed. I love you, Lissa. We all do."

"I love you guys, too." After her whispered response, the line went dead.

For several seconds, Amy continued to hold the receiver. Then slowly she returned it to the cradle and eased back into bed, bone weary.

Wallace's health, the Hamilton family scandals, Bryan's reappearance in her life— each of those events had chipped away at her peace of mind, leaving her tense and unsettled. Now she had Melissa's devastating news to contend with.

As Amy closed her eyes, she yearned for the oblivion of slumber. Prayed for it, even. But in her heart she knew that it was going to be yet another long, sleepless night.

Amy Hamilton looked tired. No, more than tired. She looked stressed-out and on edge and exhausted.

That was Bryan's conclusion as he cast a discreet glance in her direction during the nine-o'clock Sunday morning service.

His decision to return to church had met with such a positive response from his father and Dylan that he was glad he'd decided to spend an hour a week with the Lord, even if he didn't expect to get much out of it. At least he *had* been glad until he'd found out that his father planned to switch from the evening worship to the morning service. The same one the Hamilton family attended.

"I never did like going to church on Sunday night," his father had explained. "Always seemed like an afterthought to me, and the Lord deserves better than that. But I didn't have a choice before, not with my work schedule. Now that I do, I want to start my day with the Lord on Sunday."

Although James had sounded sincere, Bryan had wondered about his motivations. Was his father playing matchmaker? Trying to arrange things so Amy and his son would cross paths?

If so, it wasn't working today. Amy appeared to be lost in thought throughout much of the service—there in body but not spirit. She seemed unaware of her surroundings, and he doubted she'd even noticed his presence. Although Wallace was home from the hospital, he wasn't in the family group that had gathered for worship, Bryan noted. Had he taken a turn for the worse? Was that the reason for Amy's troubled expression?

Since he couldn't answer that question, nor explain why her distress bothered him, he tried to focus on something else. The minister, who had led the singing with gusto, had launched into his sermon, and even though Bryan wasn't all that interested in the message, he figured it might distract him.

As Bryan turned his attention to the sanctuary, he noted that Reverend Abernathy was nothing like the pastor he remembered from his school days—an older man with the quiet, thoughtful manner of a scholar, who had given well-written, well-researched sermons that informed, even if they didn't inspire.

By contrast, this minister crackled with enthusiasm. His open face, bright red hair and sprinkling of freckles gave him an approachable, boy-next-door appearance. Though a big man, he looked fit and youthful—fortyish, Bryan estimated. But his appearance was more than a little misleading. As the pastor launched into his sermon, he spoke with such authority and passion that Bryan didn't even have to try to pay attention. The man commanded it.

Although he'd missed the opening, Bryan tuned in now. Just in time to hear a message that, by odd coincidence, seemed written for him.

"…easy to get upset with those who disappoint us. Even the Lord displayed anger on occasion. Remember His visit to the temple, when He overturned the tables of the merchants and money changers? Of course, His was a righteous anger, designed to draw attention in a dramatic manner to behavior not in keeping with the principles of our faith. Such anger serves a larger purpose. It isn't provoked by hurt pride or selfishness or ego.

"Yet so much of the anger in our lives is sourced from these less-than-admirable qualities, even though we often try to convince ourselves that it's rooted in righteousness. We want to believe our anger is justified and that the other person is wrong. But often we mislead ourselves. As the Lord also reminds us in Matthew, it's easy for us to see the speck in our brother's eye, yet overlook the beam in our own. To place fault elsewhere.

"I'll be the first to admit that anger can be hard to deal with. And I speak from experience. You may believe me when I tell you that I have the temper to go with my red hair. Taming it has been one of my great challenges. But today's reading from Matthew has been a great inspiration for me, as I hope it is for all of you. In just a few words, it tells us the consequences of anger. 'But I say to you that everyone who is angry with his brother shall be liable to judgment.' And it offers us instruction about how to deal with those we have alienated, reminding us that before seeking God, 'go first to be reconciled to thy brother.'

"The directions are clear. Yet they aren't always easy to follow. Anger is a powerful emotion, one that can be difficult to control. And one that can have a profound impact on our life. It can alienate us from those we love, trap us in a cage of our own making, embitter our hearts and prevent us from realizing the destiny God has offered us.

"On this beautiful late summer day, I'd like to offer a suggestion. Find a quiet spot and open your hearts and souls to the cleansing peace of the Lord. If you're angry about anything, set it aside, if only for a moment. When you do, your heart will open and you'll experience a preview of heaven, where harmony reigns and love rules. My guess is that you won't want to pick up the anger again. And if you call on the Lord for help, if you rely on His strength, you might even find that you can walk away and leave it behind forever. For with God, all things are possible. Now let us pray."

As the minister called for the Lord's blessing on the congregation, Bryan bowed his head. He knew all about anger. For the past five-and-a-half years much of his had been directed at the Lord as he'd railed against Him for calling Darlene home and leaving him alone, mired in grief, to raise his son as a single parent. He'd always understood, on an intellectual level, that bad things could happen to good people. He'd accepted that, believing that when we don't understand the events in our lives, we're called upon to place our trust in the Lord and to know that even in our darkest hours, He is by our side.

At least he'd believed that until his convictions had been put to the test. Then his once-strong faith had faltered. He was still a believer, but anger had gotten in the way of his relationship with God. He'd turned away, closing off communication, hardening his heart against any overtures God might be making to him. Although he'd sought comfort elsewhere, even dabbling in New Age philosophy, the quest had been futile. Deep inside, he knew that the true source of consolation lay only in one place. Maybe, as the minister had said, it was time to lay aside his anger and open his heart to God's message.

And maybe it was time to open his heart to other messages, as well. In the past twenty-four hours many of his long-held convictions about Amy had been shaken. He'd already begun to suspect that she'd changed. That had been confirmed in the parking lot yesterday. Then his brother had hinted that she still cared for him. His dad had suggested he consider her as a new partner. He wasn't sure about any of that. But perhaps it was time to set his anger aside and think long and hard about his feelings for the woman he'd once loved.

Ten years ago, when she'd asked for space, he'd interpreted that as a rejection, assumed she didn't love him. But perhaps, as Kevin had suggested, she hadn't meant that at all. Maybe her feelings had been stronger than he realized; strong enough that they'd scared her because she wasn't yet ready to make the kind of commitment Bryan wanted. Perhaps, if he'd been more patient, if he'd tried to understand how her perspective had been shaped by a far different upbringing than his, their story might have had a happy ending. Instead, feeling rejected, his pride bruised, he'd backed off. And in time, he'd loved another.

Bryan had no regrets about his marriage to Darlene. She'd been a wonderful wife, and she'd given him a son who was the light of his life. But suddenly he did have regrets about the way his relationship with Amy had ended. And for the first time, he wondered if the fault might be as much his as it was hers.

As the congregation rose and began to sing the final hymn, Bryan's thoughts drifted back to his senior year in high school. When he and

Amy had first begun to date on a steady basis, it had seemed like a dream come true to him. After admiring her from afar for three years, he'd found it difficult to believe that someone like her—outgoing, smart, pretty, socially prominent—would ever fall for a quiet, introspective guy like him, from the other side of the river. Perhaps, on a subconscious level, he'd been waiting all along for the proverbial ax to fall. Expecting it, even. So in their first year of college, when she'd said, "I need some space," he'd heard *I don't love you anymore*. He'd been hurt and angry, but more resigned than surprised. She was a Hamilton, after all. To think that anything serious could ever develop between them was…well, it was just a fairy tale.

In truth, perhaps it had been, back in those days, before they'd both had a chance to grow up a little more. But Kevin didn't seem to think it was now. Nor did his father. And if he looked deep in his soul, if he put aside his anger and wounded pride, Bryan didn't, either. Kevin was right. There was something in Amy's eyes when she looked at him that suggested her feelings still ran deep. Perhaps they'd been subdued through the years. Buried in the ashes of their youthful parting.

Yet it was possible that beneath the ashes, embers still glowed, waiting to be fanned back to life, as his father had hinted. In her heart—as well as his.

It was too soon to consider testing that theory, of course. Despite his new insights, despite the minister's sermon, Bryan still had issues to deal with. He couldn't just dismiss the feelings he'd harbored in his heart for such a long time. All these years he'd thought he had been the wronged party in their breakup. That if Amy could put him off with such ease, she mustn't love him. That she'd put a higher priority on career than on family. The notion that he might have been wrong rattled him. As did the possibilities that suddenly seemed to open before him if he *was* at fault, if she did still care for him. In fact, he wasn't only rattled, but scared. He felt lost, and clueless about how to proceed in this uncharted territory.

Then the words of the song being sung by the congregation penetrated his consciousness, and he knew, deep in his soul, that he didn't have to face his dilemma alone. Help was available. He had only to ask. As those seated around him launched into the final line of the hymn, he added his voice to theirs.

"'Help of the helpless, Lord abide with me.'"

* * *

"Way to go, champ!"

Too intent to respond to his father's compliment, Dylan maneuvered the remote-controlled boat around the last obstacle in Sugar Tree Lake, then aimed it in their direction. As it glided toward shore, his posture relaxed and he tilted his head back, grinning at Bryan. "This is cool, Dad."

"I had a boat kind of like that when I was your age. But it took me a lot longer to figure out how to control it. By the time I did, the hull bore quite a few battle scars from close encounters with rocks."

Dylan's grin widened. "Ms. Patterson says I have good hand-eye carnation."

Chuckling, Bryan reached over and tousled Dylan's hair. "I think you mean coordination. And she's right. You're already a whiz with the mouse on the computer. I can't keep up with you."

"Maybe your fingers don't work as good because you're older," Dylan offered in a matter-of-fact tone.

"Now there's an uplifting thought." A wry smile lifted the corners of Bryan's mouth. "But I think I still have a few good years left. Do you want to try this again?"

"Sure. But let's find a new spot." Dylan scanned the lake as Bryan leaned down to lift the miniature cruiser from the water. "Hey, look! It's Ms. Hamilton!"

At Dylan's enthusiastic news bulletin, Bryan almost went headfirst into the lake. Tottering, he snagged the boat, then regained his balance. As he stood, he followed the direction of Dylan's finger. Across the lake, a woman in running shoes, hot-pink shorts and a tank top was jogging. And she was heading their way. Her hair was pulled back with some kind of pink scrunchy thing, and her attention was focused on the walkway in front of her, meaning she was unaware of their presence. It was Amy, all right. He'd recognize those long legs anywhere, as well as her blond hair and lithe form. But what was she doing here *now*? Since his father had said they'd run into her after the evening service, he'd figured it would be safe to bring Dylan in the early afternoon.

He'd figured wrong.

Just as he was debating the merits of trying to make a fast escape, Dylan nixed that possibility.

"Hey, Ms. Hamilton! Hi!"

As his son's excited voice rang across the water, Amy looked up. When she saw them, her step faltered, as if she, too, was thinking about turning around and running the other way. In the end, though, she regained her rhythm, though she slowed her pace. Almost as if she was putting the encounter off as long as possible.

When she drew close, she dropped back to a walk. Her face was flushed, but whether from the run or the surprise of the impromptu encounter, Bryan couldn't tell. All he knew was that she looked…different today. It could be her attire, he reasoned. At work, she wore classy, tailored clothing and maintained a brisk, businesslike, professional attitude. In her casual running clothes, she seemed softer, somehow. And vulnerable. Not to mention appealing.

"Hi, Dylan. Bryan." Amy spared Bryan a quick glance, noting the boat in his hands, before returning her attention to the little boy. "How's the sailing?"

"Great! Dad says I'm doing real good. You want to see my ship?"

"Sure."

Turning, Dylan reached for the boat and proceeded to point out all the details. Amy's enthusiastic reaction seemed to please him. "Dad gave it to me last night. You want to sail it?"

"I'm afraid I don't know how."

"It's easy. I can show you." He set the boat in the water and picked up the remote control. For a second he seemed confused by the various dials. "I've only done this once," he told Amy. "You show her, okay, Dad?" He thrust the remote at Bryan.

Short of appearing rude, Bryan didn't see that he had a choice. But a quick look at Amy's face confirmed that she felt just as awkward about this as he did. After an abbreviated explanation, he passed the remote to her as fast as he could, trying to ignore the brush of her slender fingers against his as she grasped the control panel.

For a couple of minutes, under Dylan's animated direction, she sent the boat in various directions. As she negotiated a wide turn, Dylan looked up at her. "We're going to get some ice cream. Do you want some, too?"

"Not today. I'm having dinner in a little while, and I don't want to ruin my appetite."

"We're eating later. Grandpa's cooking spaghetti. What are you having?"

"I don't know. I'm going to my Mom and Dad's house with my brothers and sister, and Mom didn't tell me the menu." Changing the subject, she pointed across the lake, where a duck was casting a suspicious eye on the approaching boat. "Look, Dylan. He's trying to figure out who the intruder is."

So the monthly Hamilton family Sunday dinner was still a tradition, Bryan reflected, casting an idle glance toward the duck. Some things never changed. In a sense, that was a—

"Dad. Dad!"

The insistent voice of his son penetrated his consciousness at last, and he looked down. "What is it, champ?"

"Jeff's here." He pointed to a youngster near the gazebo. "He's in my class. Can I show him my boat?"

"Sure. But stay where I can see you."

"Okay."

Dylan took off at a run, and only then did Bryan realize his mistake. Now he was alone with Amy. And his memories of this place. *Their* place. Did she even recall how special it had once been to them? he wondered.

It had all started after he'd helped her salvage her yearbook files. They'd begun to talk more, even sharing an occasional lunch in the cafeteria. When the yearbook had finally been published, she'd presented him with the first copy and invited him to the Bakeshoppe to celebrate after school. After ordering hot-fudge sundaes to go, she'd suggested they walk over to the park and enjoy their treat by the lake. He hadn't argued. He would have followed Amy to the ends of the earth.

They had been so busy laughing and chatting that neither had noticed the dark clouds scuttling across the sky. Their first clue that the weather had changed was the fat drop of water that plopped on the bench between them, leaving a dark splotch on the wood.

Only then had Bryan looked up and realized they were in for a sudden spring downpour. Grabbing her hand, he'd pulled her to her feet and tugged her toward the gazebo. "Let's make a run for it."

But she hadn't budged. Surprised, he'd turned back to her. As the clouds opened, she'd tilted her laughing face toward the sky.

"I love the rain, don't you?" she'd said, her expression joyous. "It washes everything clean and makes the world fresh and new again."

Despite the intensifying rain, Bryan had been riveted to the spot. Almost the exact spot in which they were now standing, he realized. Back then, all the longing that he'd kept bottled up inside for three long years had surged to the surface. When she'd looked at him, the rain clinging to her eyelashes, the laughter had faded from her face. He'd known then that he was going to kiss her, and her expression had told him she knew it, too. He had lifted his hand to her face, and for a brief second she'd seemed taken aback. Then surprise had softened to warmth—and welcome. She'd swayed toward him—and the rest was history.

Now Bryan searched her face, wondering if she remembered the sweet intensity of that first kiss. And then he had the most absurd thought...what would happen if he did the same thing right now? Touched her face, leaned toward her for a kiss? Would she respond or recoil?

As Bryan looked at her, Amy found his expression hard to read—and she was too off balance to even try. Being in this place, with this man, was wreaking havoc on her emotional equilibrium. Sugar Tree Park had held a special place in her heart ever since she and Bryan had shared their first kiss here, in the midst of a rainstorm. For weeks before that, from the time he'd helped her salvage the yearbook, Bryan Healey had captivated her. It hadn't taken her long to recognize something special in the quiet young man: a tender heart, and a depth that was lacking in most of the guys she'd dated. Unlike them, he seemed able to look beyond her blond hair, cheerleader image and red sports car, and to appreciate her intellect, her aspirations, and all of the qualities that made her who she was as a person, not as the daughter of the town's most prominent and wealthy citizen. That had touched her heart and endeared him to her in a way nothing else could have, paving the way for the romance that followed.

Of course, that was a long time ago. Bryan had moved on, fallen in love with someone else, married. She meant nothing to him anymore. Yet, as she looked at him now, something seemed to flicker to life in his eyes. Something that she couldn't quite identify. But it reminded her of that day long ago, when his eyes had darkened as he'd signaled his intent to kiss her.

A sudden, unexpected yearning swept over her, so intense that for a second she could hardly breathe. Yet even as her heart began to bang against her rib cage, Amy berated herself for her overactive imagination. Whatever she thought she'd seen in Bryan's eyes had surely just been wishful thinking on her part. Hadn't it?

The silence between them lengthened to the point of being uncomfortable. Someone needed to say something. Shifting her weight from one foot to the other, Amy brushed a few stray strands of hair back from her face and checked her watch. "Well...I need to get home or I'll be late for dinner."

Several more beats of silence passed. Bryan swallowed hard before he responded, but his voice still sounded husky when he spoke. "Where are you living these days?"

"The Enclave."

Her car might have surprised him; her residence didn't. The upscale, six-story condo within walking distance of Hamilton Media was the "in" place to live among young singles. The units were reported to be pricey and pretentious, though Bryan had no first-hand knowledge of the building. Few folks from Hickory Mills had ever been inside. The top of the structure was visible to his left, a few blocks away, and he turned in that direction. "I should have guessed. At least you don't have far to go."

When she didn't reply, he turned back to her. She seemed about to say something, but then a resigned look settled over her face and she broke eye contact. "Tell Dylan I said goodbye, okay?" Turning, she set off at a jog down the path toward home—and away from him.

There had been a time when Bryan had

been very good about masking his feelings, at keeping his expression neutral and noncommittal. But for some reason, that skill seemed to desert him when he was around Amy. Just now, it had been clear she'd come to the conclusion that Bryan felt his long-held opinion of her had been validated because of her choice of residence. In fact, though, he didn't feel that way at all. It was just that nothing had been going as he'd expected recently, and it had been a relief to find one thing about her that didn't surprise him.

Still, if she thought otherwise, maybe it was for the best. He needed time to regroup, to sort through his emotions and his assumptions. He couldn't move forward until he felt more settled.

Unfortunately, he had the disturbing feeling that waiting wasn't going to be an option. Things were moving too fast. And he suspected the pace was only going to accelerate.

Chapter Seven

As Amy turned into the long driveway leading to her childhood home, she slowed the car and surveyed the stately red-brick, three-story Greek Revival house that had been in the Hamilton family for three generations. Set back on a wide lawn, its serene, classical symmetry conveyed a feeling of permanence and stability and order, and its sheltering walls beckoned, seeming to offer a promise of haven, tranquility and calm.

Back in high school, one of her classmates had told Amy that the Hamilton house looked like a place where you could escape from the world, that within its protective walls a person could find safety and solace. It had been a romantic notion, and back then Amy had thought of her home that way, too. But time had taught her that no physical structure could offer protection from conflict or hurt or pain or emotional trauma. God was the only one who could grant that kind of refuge. A familiar verse from Psalms played in her mind: "Only in God be at rest, my soul, for from Him comes my hope." She'd taken that to heart long ago, and it had given her great comfort during the recent trials her family had endured.

Once she came to a stop in front of the house, Amy took an inventory of the cars lining the circular driveway. Heather and Ethan were already here, as was Heather's twin, Chris. Tim hadn't arrived yet, but that didn't surprise her. Always a workaholic, the man had become even more driven since taking Jeremy's place at the helm of Hamilton Media. He'd no doubt rush in at the last minute. But she knew he'd show up. The monthly family dinner was a tradition none of the siblings ever missed. Especially now, with Wallace finally home from the hospital. Despite his frail appearance, seeing him back at the head of the table would help make life seem more normal—something they all needed right now.

The front door, with its ornate leaded-glass window, was unlocked, as it always was for these Sunday afternoon dinners. Amy pushed through into the central hall, but the voices drifting from the back of the house told her that the family had gathered on the terraced patio. She headed in that direction, stopping for a brief second at the rear door to take in the scene. To most people, it would appear to be a typical lazy-afternoon family gathering. Her father sat on a chaise lounge, his silver hair glinting in the late-afternoon sun. He smiled as he exchanged a word with his wife of thirty-five years, Nora. Petite, with large hazel eyes, she could pass for half her age if it wasn't for the silver flecks in her shoulder-length golden hair. Heather sat close by, Ethan behind her with his hands on her shoulders. Chris stood a bit apart, watching the scene as he sipped a glass of minted iced tea.

Yes, to an outsider the scene would look relaxed. But Amy knew otherwise. For one thing, her father never sat, except at mealtime. He was always on the go, with more energy than he sometimes knew what to do with. Since his illness, however, his vigor had declined, forcing him to adopt a slower pace. Once robust, he'd lost a fair amount of weight, and his perennial tan had faded to an unhealthy pallor.

There were changes in her mother, too. More flecks of silver in her hair. A few new lines on her forehead. Dark shadows beneath her eyes. As she gripped her husband's hand, the placid smile on her face couldn't quite mask her deeper anxiety, which swirled just under the surface like the unsettled rumblings of an earthquake still contained belowground. Heather had pulled up her wrought-iron chair to within inches of her father, and she was perched on the edge of her seat, the taut lines of her body conveying her stress. As for Chris…minted iced tea had always been his "comfort" drink. He never touched it unless he was stressed-out.

No question about it. The past few months had taken an obvious toll on her family.

"Amy! I didn't see you! How are you, dear?" Nora rose and moved toward her oldest daughter, enfolding her in a warm hug.

"Good, Mom." Amy returned the embrace, then moved beside her father and bent down to kiss his forehead. "Hi, Dad. You're looking good."

"It's nice to be home. If I never see another hospital in my life, it will be too soon."

After greeting Heather and Ethan, Amy turned to Chris. "Where's Felicity?"

"Working. Some hot story was breaking at the *Dispatch*. She said she'd stop by later if she could."

The romance between Chris and Felicity was one of the few bright spots in the current Hamilton saga. And Amy endorsed the union. Felicity would be a good addition to the family. A top-notch reporter, she was also beautiful, intelligent and strong. Felicity was a woman who understood that everyone marched to the beat of their own drummer, and encouraged them to do so. In other words, she was a perfect match for Chris.

"Miss Nora, dinner's ready."

The group assembled on the terrace turned toward Vera Mae, who stood in the doorway, her hands on her ample hips. She'd been the housekeeper and sometimes-cook at the Hamilton house for as long as Amy could remember. And she'd looked the same for as long as Amy could remember, too. She always wore a voluminous white apron with deep pockets—where she'd often stashed pieces of candy for the children when they were small—and her long brown hair, streaked with gray, was braided, then coiled on top of her head. She had merry green eyes with a fan of lines at the corners, and a hearty, uninhibited laugh that never failed to bring a smile to Amy's face. After all these years, the Hamiltons thought of her more like family than hired help. And, after being widowed at a young age, she'd treated them as such, fussing and worrying over them as if they were her own, even volunteering to give up her day of rest to prepare a special celebratory family dinner to welcome Wallace home from the hospital.

Frowning, Nora checked her watch. "Tim's not here yet. I hate to start without him."

"He'll be along soon, Mom," Amy reassured her. "I don't think he'd want us to wait."

"He probably got caught up at the office," Heather offered as she stood.

"He's working on Sunday?" Wallace swung his legs to the ground, taking Nora's arm to steady himself as he rose.

Distressed at the slip, Heather tucked her hair behind her ear and sent Amy a guilty look. Hard as their father worked, he'd always reserved Sundays for the Lord and for family. They'd all followed his example until the recent upheaval at Hamilton Media. Tim hadn't told his father about his weekend hours, though.

"He just wants to do a good job, Dad," Amy stepped in. "Being thrust into the top position with no warning had to be a shock. There's a lot to learn, and that takes some extra time. I'm sure things will settle down soon."

Leading the way toward the house, Wallace conceded the point. "Considering the circumstances, I guess that's true. This illness has played havoc with everything."

"But you're doing better, Dad. That's the main thing," Heather encouraged.

As they settled themselves at the enormous, handmade table in the dining room, designed to accommodate the whole family as well as a good number of guests, Vera Mae began delivering brimming serving platters from the kitchen. The feast included fried chicken, from-scratch biscuits, mashed potatoes and gravy, green beans and a heaping bowl of salad.

"Eat hearty now," Vera Mae instructed. "Especially you, Mr. Wallace. You need to get some meat back on those bones."

Grinning, he reached for a biscuit. "I'll do my best."

The front door slammed, and everyone turned in unison toward the hall. Tim dashed by the doorway, then backtracked when he realized the family was already at the table. A flush crept up his neck as he entered the room and took the chair beside Amy. "Sorry I'm late."

"You're just in time for grace," Nora told him. "Wallace?"

They all joined hands and bowed their heads as Wallace offered a blessing.

"Lord, we thank You for this food, and for the comfort and love of family. We ask You to give us strength and courage as we face the trials that have come our way, and we thank You for the gift of Your presence, which lights our journey even on our darkest days. Amen."

As they dug into the meal, the conversation flowed, moving with ease from one topic to another, punctuated by laughter and teasing and friendly debate. Amy could almost pretend that this was just like any other carefree, pre-problems Sunday dinner. Until Vera Mae came to the door and sent a cautious look toward Nora.

"Miss Nora, there's a phone call for you."

"Just take a message, Vera Mae," Wallace instructed. "I don't want to interrupt dinner. It's the only time all month when we're together."

When the woman hesitated, Nora sent her a questioning look. "What is it, Vera Mae?"

"I wouldn't interrupt, except I thought you might want to take this particular call."

"Why?"

After a brief hesitation, the woman responded. "It's Jeremy."

Everyone stopped eating. Wallace's lips settled into a thin line, and a muscle twitched in his jaw. "If he wants to talk to his mother, he should come to Sunday dinner."

The four siblings exchanged uneasy looks, and Amy noted that her mother's face had lost some of its color. Wallace still didn't know Jeremy had left town in search of his fraternal grandparents, and the family had agreed that in light of Wallace's precarious health, it would be best not to share that piece of information yet. It would only upset him.

"Wallace, dear, I think I'll take it, if you don't mind. Perhaps it's something important. I won't be a minute."

Giving a stiff nod, he reached for his water glass. "Whatever you think best."

Quiet descended on the table during Nora's absence. Amy knew Tim was still angry at Jeremy for jumping ship in the midst of all the other crises they faced, and she could feel him seething beside her. Chris looked concerned, and Heather appeared distraught. Wallace's face was stony as he shoved a green bean around on his plate.

True to her word, Nora slipped back into her seat a couple of minutes later. "Jeremy says hello to everyone."

"Humph," was Wallace's only comment.

Ever since she'd arrived, Amy had been trying to figure out how to broach the subject of her phone conversation with Melissa. And how to avoid the inevitable questions her announcement would generate. She didn't want to lie to her family, but she'd promised Melissa she'd keep her secret. She'd just have to wing it, she supposed. And now seemed to be the time, considering the pall that had fallen over the table. Maybe it would distract everyone from the problems with Jeremy.

Taking a deep breath, she forced a bright tone into her voice. "I have some good news."

"We could use some," Tim muttered.

She ignored him. "I had a phone call from Melissa last night."

"Where is she?"

"Did she say when she's coming home?"

"Is she okay?"

"Did you tell her her job at the *Dispatch* is still waiting for her?"

At the barrage of questions, Amy held up her hands. "Wait. One at a time. But first let me tell you what I know. She's in Detroit. For the moment, anyway. It sounds like she's on the move with the band. I think she's considering coming home, but she's not ready to make that decision yet. She sends her love and promised to keep in touch."

"So she's with that Dean character, as we suspected?" Wallace said.

"Yes."

"He may be scum, but at least he doesn't have a record," Chris offered.

"That doesn't make me feel a whole lot better," Wallace retorted.

"Did she seem upset, Amy?" Worry clouded Nora's face.

That question moved her onto tricky ground. It was time for evasive maneuvers. "I think she misses us. And she sounded more grown-up than I can ever recall."

"It's about time," Tim groused.

"We're in a good mood today, aren't we?" Amy sent Tim a chastising look.

"Sorry."

"Is there a problem at the office?" Wallace queried.

"Nothing I can't handle." He gave a dismissive shrug. Then he turned his attention back to Amy. "Why do you think Melissa might come home?"

"I sensed that her attraction for Dean may be waning." Amy framed her response with care.

"Did she say when she'd call again?" Amy

noted Nora's white-knuckled grip on her water glass as she asked the question, and her heart ached for all her mother had endured in the past few months.

"No, Mom. It didn't sound like it would be too long, though."

"But…why didn't she call *me*?" Nora's face reflected puzzlement—and hurt.

That was another question Amy couldn't answer. "It was late when she called. Maybe she didn't want to wake you," Amy hedged.

"I wouldn't have cared if it was three in the morning. It would have been good to hear her voice." Nora's wistful tone tightened Amy's throat.

Reaching for his wife's hand, Wallace enfolded her delicate fingers in a comforting grip. "At least she's been in touch. That's a good sign. We should be thankful that she seems to be coming to her senses. And trust that the Lord will bring her safely home."

"You're right, of course. I'm sure Pastor Abernathy would remind me of the same thing. Such a nice man. And he gives wonderful sermons." Nora composed her face and managed to dredge up a smile.

"I'm looking forward to going back to church as soon as I regain my strength," Wallace said.

"Speaking of church…I noticed Bryan and his son at services this morning. Dylan's even cuter in person than in the photos, isn't he?" Heather directed her question to her sister.

Amy stared at her. "Bryan was at church?"

Surprise flickered across Heather's face. "Yes. Didn't you notice?"

"Bryan who, dear?" Nora asked Heather.

"Bryan Healey. You remember, Mom. He dated Amy when they were in high school."

"Oh, of course. Such a nice boy. I thought he moved away years ago."

"He did. But when his wife died, he came back home with his son. In fact, we hired him a few weeks ago at *Nashville Living* as a feature writer."

"How interesting. You never told me that, Amy."

A flush began to creep up Amy's neck. Talk about going from the frying pan into the fire! The last thing she wanted to do was discuss Bryan Healey with her family. "It was no big deal, Mom. We had an opening, he had the qualifications, so we offered him the job. We hire people all the time."

"Not ex-boyfriends."

"That was a long time ago."

"I remember Bryan," Chris joined in.

"Nice guy. Seemed trustworthy. Not like some of those hotshots you dated who looked like they wanted to get you in the back seat of the car as soon as the house was out of sight."

"Thanks a lot." Amy scowled at him.

"Hey, I've been there. Male teenage hormones are a force to be reckoned with. Consider it a compliment that I thought you had the good sense to pick Bryan as a boyfriend."

"He still seems like he has a good head on his shoulders," Ethan added. "I'm just glad I claimed Heather before he arrived back in town." He reached over and squeezed his fiancée's hand.

Turning to him, a soft smile lit her face. "I always liked Bryan. But I *love* you."

"It's getting pretty deep in here, if you ask me. There are other things in life besides love, you know." Tim helped himself to another biscuit.

"Don't knock it until you've given it a try," Chris replied.

"I know all about love. I love my job, don't I?"

Rolling her eyes, Heather gave Tim a dismayed look. "You're hopeless. Is there no romance in your soul?"

"Hey, why are you ganging up on me? Amy hasn't fallen for all that romance stuff, either."

"Yet."

At Heather's cryptic comment, Amy angled a suspicious look in her direction. But before she could respond, Vera Mae pushed through the swinging door that led to the kitchen, carrying a huge, homemade apple pie fresh from the oven. That was enough to divert everyone's attention, and Amy was thankful for the timing. She didn't want to talk any more about Bryan. Not until she had some time to think things through, to reflect on Heather's surprising announcement that he'd been in church this morning. And to wrestle into submission the longing he'd stirred up in her heart this afternoon at the park.

Thankfully, the subject of Bryan didn't come up again, nor did Melissa or Jeremy. But as she prepared to leave, she pulled her mother aside, curious about the earlier phone call from her oldest brother.

"Is everything all right with Jeremy, Mom?" She kept her voice subdued so her father wouldn't overhear.

A look of distress flashed across Nora's face. "As well as can be expected, I guess. He's angry and confused and hurt. I suppose we should have told him years ago, but…well, that's water under the bridge now. At least he hasn't shut us out."

"Is he having any luck finding his grandparents?"

"No. But he has a lead he's going to follow, in Florida. If he does find the Andersons, they'll be as shocked as he was by the news. They have no idea their son had a child. I guess I should have tried harder to find them when Paul died, but I didn't have much to work with. He was estranged from his parents, and since he never spoke about them I had no idea where to look. I wish now I'd made more of an effort. Then maybe all this could have been avoided."

Tears glistened in Nora's eyes, and Amy reached over to give her a comforting hug. "It's not your fault, Mom. You did what you thought was best at the time, under very trying and emotional circumstances. No one blames you."

"Wallace and I always thought it would be better to keep the secret. I know, deep in his heart, your father regrets the fact that he let it slip at the hospital. But he was so sick, and so worried about the business…"

"We'll get through this, Mom," Amy encouraged when her mother's voice trailed off.

"I know we will. And one of these days *all* of your children will be back around this table, like before. Just wait and see."

"I'd like to believe that. It's certainly what I'm praying for."

"Me, too." Amy leaned over and kissed her mother. "I'll stop by again tomorrow."

"Thank you, dear. And keep those prayers going."

"I will." With a wave, Amy slipped through the front door and walked to her car. As she slid behind the wheel, she took another look at the house that had once rung with laughter. In her heart, she believed it would again. She *had* to believe that. But she also knew that it would take all of their combined prayers—and then some— to restore harmony to the Hamilton home.

"Mr. Hamilton?" The voice on the other end of the phone sounded surprised. "This is Russ Jackson, the security guard at The Enclave. How are you feeling, sir?"

It seemed like the whole world knew about his health problems, Wallace thought in resignation. "Holding my own, thank you," he responded. "What can I do for you?"

There was a hesitation before the man spoke. "Is Mrs. Hamilton at home?"

"No, I'm sorry. She ran into town. Is there something I can help you with?"

"Well...I hate to bother you with this."

"I don't mind at all. I have plenty of time on my hands these days."

"Thank you." The man sounded relieved. "There's a plumbing problem of some kind in Jeremy's unit. A water stain has appeared on the ceiling in the lobby, and it's growing. I tried Amy and Tim at their offices, but their voice mail kicked in. We'd like to get someone's permission before we go into his unit."

"If there's an emergency, I'm sure Jeremy would want you to take care of it. But if you'd feel more comfortable, just wait and ask him yourself." He consulted his watch. "It's pretty late. I would think he'd be there soon."

"Oh. I didn't realize he was coming back today."

"Back? Back from where?"

"I'm not sure, sir." The man was beginning to sound uncertain.

"How long has he been gone?"

"About three weeks."

Silence greeted the man's response as Wallace digested that news.

"Sir? Are you still there?"

Clearing his throat, Wallace spoke again,

though his voice wasn't quite steady. "Yes. You have my permission to take care of the plumbing problem. Don't wait for Jeremy."

"All right. Thank you, sir. And I hope your recovery is speedy."

Still stunned by the news that Jeremy had left Davis Landing, Wallace groped for a chair and eased himself down. All this time, he'd thought the boy was just lying low. Not that he'd blamed him. Having that kind of bombshell dropped on you would send anyone reeling. But he'd had no idea Jeremy had left town. The question was, where had he gone?

The sound of the kitchen door opening caught Wallace's attention, and he struggled to stand again. The last thing he wanted to do was add to Nora's worry, and seeing him slumped in a chair would bring that look of panic to her face that always tore at his gut. The increasing weakness and fatigue he'd been feeling was surely just an aftermath of the transplant. He'd ask Dr. Strickland about it at his next checkup, but in the meantime he didn't need to burden anyone with that concern. He'd be seeing the doctor in two weeks, and the man could answer his questions then. In the meantime, though, he wanted some answers to other questions. About Jeremy.

When Nora passed the library, she seemed surprised to see him standing by his desk. "Wallace! You're not working, are you?"

"No. The phone rang as I walked by the door, so I picked it up in here."

"Anything important?"

"It was a security guard from The Enclave."

"Whatever did he want?"

"There's a plumbing problem in Jeremy's apartment. He wanted authorization to go in, and he couldn't reach Amy or Tim."

A flicker of unease swept across Nora's face. "Did you give him permission?"

"Yes…after he told me that Jeremy had left town at least three weeks ago and that he didn't know when he planned to return."

Some of the color faded from Nora's face, but she remained silent.

"Do you want to tell me what this is all about?" The turbulent look on Wallace's face was at odds with his calm, composed tone.

Lifting a hand to her throat, Nora took a deep breath. She'd always been open and honest with her husband, right from the beginning. Even about Jeremy. She'd only kept this from him because she hadn't wanted to jeopardize his health by adding to his stress. But she could see now that it had been a mistake.

She should have known that it would just be a matter of time before someone let the news slip. He should have heard about Jeremy's quest from her.

Moving into the room, Nora drew close and laid a hand on his arm, her gaze seeking his, willing him to see that her intentions had been good. "I didn't think you needed that worry on top of everything else," she said softly. "But I should have told you. Jeremy went in search of the Andersons."

Wallace's face grew pasty, and his tone was flat when he spoke. "He wants to know about his real father."

"You *are* his real father. In every way that matters." Nora's voice was fierce.

"Maybe I was. Then I turned him against me by dropping that bombshell in his lap." Wallace's Adam's apple bobbed as he tried to swallow. "I handled that badly."

"You were sick."

"That's no excuse."

"It's a very good excuse. Jeremy will realize in time that we didn't mean to hurt him by keeping the information about his biological father a secret. That you did it for the best reasons—because you wanted him to feel like a Hamilton. To *be* a Hamilton. You love him just as much as you love any of your other children."

"That's true. But I wonder if Jeremy will ever believe that again?"

At the wistful quality in his voice, Nora put her arms around his neck and pulled him close. "He's a good man, Wallace. You raised a fine son. He'll come around in time. I know it in my heart."

The conviction in his wife's voice was firm, but Wallace wasn't as sure. If he had it to do over again, he wouldn't share the secret of Jeremy's true parentage. It was too late to take back the words now, though. All he could do was pray that Jeremy would find what he was looking for—and also find it in his heart to forgive the man he'd always called Dad.

Chapter Eight

"Heather! Conference. Amy's office. Now!"

The cryptic tone in Tim's voice as it zipped over the cubicles in the *Nashville Living* offices stopped Heather in mid-step as she headed toward the elevator. Her brother had thrown the command over his shoulder without breaking stride as he bore down on Amy's office, and Heather watched as he reached the closed door, gave a perfunctory knock—one quick, sharp rap—then entered without waiting for a response. A jolt of panic shot through her, and she almost ran to her sister's office, slipping inside just as Tim began to close the door.

When it clicked shut, he turned to his sisters. "Mom just called. She's worried about Dad."

Fighting down her own rising panic, Amy

gripped the edge of her desk, as if bracing for a blow. "What happened?"

"He didn't want to get up this morning. Said he was too tired. And he has a low-grade fever."

"Did Mom call Dr. Strickland?"

"Yes. He ordered some blood work. And he's prescribed antibiotics. There's more, too. Dad knows that Jeremy left town and is looking for the Andersons."

Dismay flooded Heather's face. "How did he find out?"

After a brief explanation, Tim planted his fists on his hips. Anger flashed in his eyes, and his lips grew taut. "It seems Jeremy is continuing to wreak havoc on the family."

"You can't blame this on him, Tim," Amy protested.

"No?" Fury nipped at his voice. "Don't you think it's just a little too coincidental that Dad starts to have health problems right after he hears about Jeremy? He was doing fine up until now. Stress isn't good for him."

"He did seem fine at dinner last Sunday. And that was only four days ago." It was clear that Heather was struggling to hold on to her composure.

"Now look, both of you." Amy's voice was firm. "This may be nothing. Let's try not to fall apart. And we can't blame Jeremy. He did what he felt he had to do. Everyone's upset, and we're all coping as best we can. We're just going to have to put the situation in God's hand and trust that He'll get us through this."

Tim made a dismissive gesture. "I haven't seen much evidence of God's benevolence or mercy in the past few months."

Their brother's lack of faith was troubling to both Heather and Amy, and the sisters exchanged a look. But now wasn't the time to try to convert him, Amy knew. She just prayed that someday he'd see the light.

"Well, let's try to stay calm until the test results are back. In the meantime, I think I'll run out to the house at lunchtime and check on Dad myself," Amy said.

"Tell him I'll be out tonight," Tim instructed.

"Me, too," Heather added.

After consulting his watch, Tim headed toward the door, speaking over his shoulder. "I have work to do. Let me know how Dad is when you get back." He exited without waiting for a response.

Turning to Heather, Amy could tell that her sister was ready to cry. She had always worn her tender heart on her sleeve. "Why don't you take a quick walk around the block? Or over to the park?" Amy suggested in a gentle tone. "You'll feel better if you get some fresh air and sunshine."

Sniffing, Heather rose. "Yeah. I think I will." She hesitated at the door, turning to look back at Amy. "Do you really think Dad will be okay?"

"I'm sure of it."

Amy managed to sound confident, and her response seemed to satisfy Heather. In truth, though, she wasn't as certain. Her father's color hadn't been good on Sunday, even before he knew about Jeremy. At the time, she'd attributed it to the shock his body had been through. Perhaps, though, it had been more than that. And perhaps not. Maybe after she saw him at lunchtime she'd feel better.

Unfortunately, Amy felt worse after her visit. Her father was up, but he seemed listless and drawn, the white bandage on his arm, where blood had been drawn a couple of hours before, a stark reminder that all might not be right. When she'd reported her visit to Heather and Tim, she'd tried to downplay her fears, deciding to let them draw their own conclusions after they went out to the house later in the day.

As for her, she sensed danger lurking close by, like the distant rumble of thunder that announces an approaching storm even before the clouds appear. But she could do nothing except pray. And hope that her unease wasn't a premonition of more problems to come.

Focus had never been a problem for Amy. At least, not until the past few weeks. However, as she stared at her computer screen, trying to compose what should have been a simple response letter to a reader, she couldn't concentrate. Though the weekend had passed without incident, she still felt unsettled and exhausted. Unlike Tim, who seemed able to function on a few hours' sleep a night, Amy needed more rest. Rest she hadn't been getting. Perhaps the good news they'd had this morning about Wallace would help. The blood cultures had come back negative, and his fever had dropped, although his energy level was still very low.

A knock on her door startled her and she jumped, yet more evidence that her nerves were on edge, she realized. Turning, she found Bryan in the doorway. In the midst of the turmoil in her life, she found his calm, solid, in-control presence somehow reassuring.

"Yes?"

"Sorry to bother you, but Heather's out. I have a bit of a problem. The school just phoned to tell me Dylan's sick. It doesn't sound like anything serious, but they think he should go home. Dad's on an overnight fishing trip, or I'd call him."

"Go pick him up," Amy said without hesitation.

"I would, except I have an interview scheduled with Dan Marconi in Nashville in forty-five minutes. He's only in town today, and I worked every angle I could to set this up. I don't want to see all that effort wasted. And I'm sure you don't want to lose the story."

Now Amy understood his dilemma. She, too, wanted this interview to come off. Heather had mentioned the upcoming visit of the reclusive hometown boy turned Pulitzer Prize-winning novelist at the last staff meeting, remarking that it would be quite a coup if the magazine could do a profile of him. When Bryan had offered to take on the challenge, no one had held out much hope that he'd manage to wrangle an audience. Yet he'd found a way.

"Could someone else do the interview?" Amy asked.

"I tried that already. I called his publicist, but was told it's either me or no one. It seems Mr. Marconi doesn't like surprises or last-minute changes."

The solution seemed obvious. At least to her. She wasn't sure how Bryan would feel about it, though. "Then why don't I pick up Dylan? If you called and authorized the school to release him to me, I could take him to your dad's house, then stay with him until you get back."

Startled, Bryan stared at her. She must want this story even more than he'd thought if she was willing to leave her office and babysit a young child for several hours. It did solve the problem, though. And even if Bryan had personal issues with the woman across from him, he knew he could trust her with his son. Besides, there didn't seem to be any other option.

"Okay. I guess that will work." The lack of enthusiasm in his voice was apparent even to him. When he continued, he tried to sound a bit more upbeat. "I'll call the school now, and I'll be back as fast I can. I already called the doctor, and I can pick up anything he might prescribe on the way home. Are you sure you don't mind interrupting your day like this?"

"No. I don't want to lose this story. And I like Dylan."

The losing-the-story part he could understand. Amy had always been single-minded and focused about her projects in school. It was logical that that commitment would carry over to her career. But the comment about Dylan surprised him. Yet the two had seemed to click when they'd been together. And Dylan liked her, too.

"All right. Just call my cell if you need me." He fished around in the pocket of his khaki slacks and withdrew a key ring, slipping off a key and handing it across the desk. "This is for the back door."

As his hand brushed hers, Amy felt an unnerving jolt of electricity. Bryan, on the other hand, seemed unaffected by the contact. But that shouldn't surprise her, based on his tepid response to her offer. Trying to ignore the hollow feeling in the pit of her stomach, she checked her watch. "You're already cutting it close."

"Yeah." Still, for several seconds he didn't move. Then he jammed the key ring back into his pocket and headed for the door. "Thanks," he said as he exited.

After cleaning up a few loose ends, Amy grabbed her purse and left her office. It wasn't until she pulled up in front of the school that her nerves kicked in. What on earth had she gotten herself into? She didn't know a thing about children, especially sick children! What if Dylan was more ill than anyone thought? What if he balked at leaving with her?

As it turned out, he wasn't and he didn't. The school nurse told her that he'd thrown up and was running a slight temperature, but she also said that a number of children were out with a mild case of the flu. For his part, Dylan seemed delighted to see her. His flushed face brightened when she appeared in the doorway of the infirmary, and when he trustingly placed his small hand in hers, Amy's throat tightened with emotion. For the first time in her life, she realized just how dependent children were on the adults in their lives to see to their needs, both physical and emotional. And she had a sudden, clear understanding of the awesome responsibility of parenthood. No wonder Melissa felt unprepared to be a mother.

By the time they arrived at the house, Dylan had nodded off, his head lolling against the seat-belt strap. His usual animation and chatter were absent, leading Amy to conclude that he was, indeed, one sick puppy. It was bed for him, and then she'd see if she could round up any soup or Jell-O or toast.

As she inserted the key in the lock and stepped inside the kitchen, a drowsy Dylan close by her side, memories came flooding back, and for just a second she was eighteen again. Eighteen and carefree and in love, with

a bright, shining future before her. She'd
known happy times in this place. In this very
room, in fact. During the spring and summer
she and Bryan were dating, she'd visited
often, many times sharing a meal at the worn
oak table that was still the centerpiece of the
kitchen. James and Catherine Healey had
always welcomed her with open arms, and
she'd felt at home in the modest frame
bungalow. Though she'd grown up in much
grander surroundings, she'd recognized at
once that the Healey and Hamilton house-
holds shared the most essential ingredient in
the recipe for a home—love.

"Can I have a drink of water, Ms. Hamilton?"

Dylan's sleepy voice interrupted her
thoughts, and she blinked back the moisture
that had misted her vision. "Of course, honey.
And why don't you call me Amy? It's much
shorter than Ms. Hamilton."

He gave her a toothy grin. "Okay."

She filled a glass with water, then took his
hand. "Show me where your bedroom is, and
we'll get you into your pajamas."

Leading the way through the living room,
he turned down a short hall and headed toward
the last room. "This is where Dad and me
sleep," he informed her.

For a second, Amy hesitated on the threshold. The room was furnished with twin beds, both neatly made, and matching bureaus stood against the wall across from each footboard. Several stuffed animals, along with a familiar-looking remote-controlled boat, were strewn across the top of one. The other was bare except for an eight-by-ten-inch framed wedding picture.

Without even thinking, Amy moved toward the photo and stared at the fleeting moment in time captured by the image. Bryan, handsome and elegant in a tux, wore an expression of deep contentment. The face of the woman beside him—pretty in a quiet, unassuming way—was joyful and radiant, her long brown hair falling in soft waves beneath a wisp of veil. They looked like a nice couple. Like they were meant for each other, Amy was forced to acknowledge. Her throat constricted, and she drew in an unsteady breath.

"That's my mom and dad on the day they got married," Dylan offered.

With an effort, Amy composed her face. "Your mom was very pretty."

After giving the photo serious consideration, Dylan nodded. "Yeah. But I don't remember her. She went to heaven right after

I was borned. Dad says she loved me a whole lot, though."

"I'm sure she did. And she still loves you, from heaven."

A wistful look stole over his face. "I wish she was here, though. Heaven is a long way away. You forget how much someone loves you if you never see them."

Yes, Amy supposed, you do. Whether they're in heaven or on earth. Her thoughts strayed to Bryan, and her youthful insistence that they needed space, and time apart. But she quickly cut off that line of thought. Right now, she had a sick little boy to take care of.

"Okay, where are your pajamas?"

After rummaging in a drawer, Dylan produced them. But as he held them up, his face suddenly grew pale. "I—I don't feel so good," he stammered.

Sensing what was about to happen, Amy reached down and urged him toward the bathroom. They almost made it, too. But just as she lifted the lid of the toilet, whatever was left in Dylan's stomach spewed out, splattering onto the tile floor, the toilet seat—and the front of her linen jacket. When the eruption subsided, Dylan was left shaky and tearful.

"I—I don't l-like throwing u-up." His words were choked by sobs as he clung to Amy.

"Oh, honey, nobody does." Amy reached up and pushed his hair back from his damp face. "But you feel better now, don't you?"

"Yeah."

"Then that's a good thing. Come on, let's get you changed and into bed, then I'll find something cool for you to drink."

Ignoring her stained jacket, she helped Dylan into his pajamas, then searched through the kitchen until she found some ginger ale to settle his stomach. While he sat on a stool in his room and sipped the soda, she headed back to the bathroom and swiped at the front of her jacket with a damp towel. However, her efforts did little to mitigate the damage or even render the garment wearable, she realized in dismay. The fabric was clinging to her uncomfortably, and she pulled it away from her skin in distaste as she headed back to the bedroom and looked around for something—anything—that could serve as a makeshift top.

"Dad has lots of shirts in the closet," Dylan offered, surprising Amy with his perceptiveness. "He wouldn't mind if you borrowed one."

The sliding door for the closet was within arm's reach, but Amy hesitated. She had a feeling Bryan wouldn't appreciate her rummaging around among his clothes. But she couldn't leave this jacket on, either. Only a trip to the dry cleaner would restore it to wearable condition. Realizing there was no other option, she reached over and slid back the closet door, determined to do this as quickly as possible. Going through someone's closet was way too…personal. And it became even more so as Bryan's unique scent enveloped her while she rifled through his shirts. When her heart tripped into double time and a surge of longing swept over her, she grabbed the next shirt she came to and shoved the closet door closed with more force than necessary. She turned to find Dylan regarding her with interest.

"You banged the door."

A flush rose on her cheeks. "I know. It just kind of…slipped."

"That happens to me sometimes, too. But Dad says it's not good to bang doors."

"He's right. I'll be more careful the next time." Not that there would ever be a next time. "I'm going to put on this shirt and clean up the bathroom, okay? You just call me if you need anything."

Wearing Bryan's shirt was even harder than looking at it in the closet, Amy discovered, as she slipped her arms through the sleeves and inhaled the scent that was uniquely his. For a second she closed her eyes and breathed in the essence of the man she had once loved. Then she forced herself to consider more practical matters. The shirt was way too big, for one thing. It would get in her way while she tried to clean the bathroom. To solve the problem, she rolled up the sleeves to the elbows, then knotted the shirttails around her waist. Better. It looked less like a man's shirt now. Though the oxford-blue cloth wasn't the best match with her pencil-slim peach-colored skirt, she noted with a wry smile. She'd win no fashion awards today.

In short order, she'd restored the bathroom to pristine condition. By the time she returned to Dylan's room, he had finished the soda and was clutching a worn teddy bear.

"All right. It's into bed for you, young man." She headed over to turn back the covers.

"That's Dad's bed."

She pulled her hand back as if she'd just received an electric shock.

"Anyway, can I lay on the sofa in the living room?" Dylan continued. "That's what Dad always lets me do when I'm sick."

Anxious to be out of the bedroom, Amy

agreed to the request at once. "Sure. Let me grab your pillow." Turning to the other bed, she reached for it, along with a throw that lay at the foot, then followed him into the living room. She plumped the pillow and he climbed up.

"Will you sit with me?"

"Of course." She settled onto the couch. Instead of laying his head on the pillow she'd tucked into the corner, however, Dylan stretched out and nuzzled onto her lap, still clutching his teddy bear. For a second Amy was taken aback. Then she reached for the throw and draped it over him, brushing the hair off his forehead with a gentle hand. In minutes, his even breathing told her that he was asleep.

Kicking off her shoes, Amy sat for a long time, stroking Dylan's hair in a comforting, repetitive gesture. The afternoon shadows lengthened, and she realized that Bryan's reluctant subject must have granted him more time than he'd expected. Not that she was surprised. Bryan was an easy person to talk with. Or had been, she corrected herself. Since his return, she'd found their conversations awkward. But no one else seemed to have that problem, including the man he was now interviewing. And that was promising. If it resulted in a better story, she didn't mind if he was a little later than planned. As long as she was on her way by five-thirty, she'd be fine. And that was still—she checked her watch—an hour and a half away. She ought to just take this opportunity to let her tense nerves unwind.

As the minutes ticked by, the silence of the house and the small warm body pressed close to hers did help her relax. She snuggled lower on the sofa, careful not to disturb Dylan, then let her head rest against the upholstered back. After a few minutes, her eyelids grew heavy, and when they drifted shut, she didn't even try to keep them open. She had never been able to sleep in the middle of the day. The best she could hope for was a light doze. But that was better than nothing. Anything that helped her get some much-needed rest would be welcome.

Juggling a large sack of Chinese food in one hand and a colorful puzzle in the other, Bryan tucked the game box under his arm and tried the back door. Open. Good. He pushed through, scanning the kitchen. Empty. And the house was quiet. Too quiet. He set the bag and box on the table as a tingle of unease raced up his spine. Dylan was no doubt sleeping, but he knew his anxiety wouldn't dissipate until he confirmed that. His tendency to worry about his son, and to be overprotective, was a legacy of Dylan's rough beginning, and something Bryan battled daily.

Striding through the living room, Bryan headed straight for the hall. He wouldn't have noticed the two figures on the couch if a ray of the setting sun hadn't peeked through the front window just then, illuminating the blond hair that was splayed across the back of the upholstered piece. At the sight, Bryan came to a dead stop.

From his position behind the couch, all he could see was Amy's hair, burnished to gold by the late-afternoon sun. Taking care to make no noise, he moved closer, then circled the couch. Her head was tipped back, her face relaxed and youthful in sleep. Only in their absence did Bryan recognize the lines of strain and tension that had tightened her features ever since his return. Etched partly by him, he was sure, but also by her father's illness and the other troubles that had beset the Hamilton family. Dylan lay sprawled across her lap, and Amy's hand rested on his arm, the gentle gesture protective even in sleep. Her discarded pumps lay at her feet, one standing, the other on its side.

Tenderness swept through his heart. In sleep, they both looked vulnerable. And they looked right together, somehow, the two of them. As if they were meant to be connected, to share a bond. Or perhaps that was just wishful thinking, Bryan speculated. Not so much related to Amy, as to the fact that more and more, he'd begun to realize that Dylan did need a mother. At least that's what he told himself.

Just then Amy stirred, almost as if she sensed his scrutiny, and her eyelids flickered open. For a second she seemed a bit disoriented as she looked at him. Then her face cleared and she transferred her attention to Dylan, who continued to sleep soundly as she laid a hand on his forehead.

"He's cooler now," she whispered.

It took Bryan a few seconds to find his voice. "Sorry I'm late. Mr. Marconi turned out to be quite a talker. And traffic was bad."

Alarmed, she checked her watch. Five o'clock. Good. She still had half an hour. "No problem. How did it go?"

"Great. I think we're going to have a good piece." He moved toward her and reached for Dylan, risking a glance at her as he bent. Her deep blue eyes, only inches from his, stared back at him and he had the feeling she'd stopped breathing. Or was it him that had suddenly become breathless?

Instead of trying to figure it out, he swept Dylan up, holding the boy close. His son stirred, and when he opened his eyes he grinned at Bryan.

"Hi, Dad."

"Hi, champ. How are you feeling?"

"Good. But I threw up again when I got home."

As Bryan and Dylan had this exchange, Amy stood. Only then did Bryan notice that she was wearing an oversize man's shirt. *His* shirt, he realized with a jolt.

Warm color flooded Amy's neck. "My jacket was a casualty. I hope you don't mind that I borrowed one of your shirts."

"It looks better on you than it does on me."

Surprised by his comment—and even more by the husky timbre of his voice—Amy's color rose higher, spilling onto her cheeks. Since she didn't have any idea how to respond to his remark, she chose to ignore it. "Can I return it next week?"

"Of course. In the meantime, I'll have your jacket cleaned."

"That's not necessary."

"I insist."

Rather than argue, she let it go. "I gave Dylan some soda earlier. I'll get him some more. It will help settle his stomach and keep him from dehydrating."

"Thanks. I'll take him into the bedroom."

"Aw, Dad, I want to stay up."

"Sorry, champ. Not tonight. You need to get better. The more you rest, the sooner that'll happen. By Sunday, you might even feel well enough to go sailing again."

The lure of an outing to the park was too hard to resist, and Dylan capitulated. "Okay, I guess." He looked over at Amy. "Will you come in and see me later?"

"Of course."

As Amy refilled Dylan's glass with ice and soda, she noticed the children's puzzle on the table. A perfect gift for a sick little boy, she reflected, impressed by Bryan's instincts and his comfortable, deft handling of Dylan. He was a natural father. But then, he'd always been competent at anything he'd tackled. An appealing quality. Even more appealing right now, however, were the enticing smells emanating from the white sack. Her rumbling stomach reminded her that she'd had only a container of yogurt for lunch, and that had been a long time ago. But she doubted whether she'd have time to eat anything until much later tonight.

"Considering how you stepped in to help today, I figured the least I could do was feed you."

At the sound of Bryan's voice, Amy looked toward the doorway. She was tempted both by the food and the opportunity to spend more time with this special man, though she doubted the latter was wise.

"Think about it while I take this in to Dylan." Bryan stepped toward her and retrieved the glass of soda, then disappeared back down the hall.

Once more, Amy considered the sack on the table. Okay, she'd stay for ten minutes, just long enough to gobble down a quick bite. She did need to eat, after all. There were practical reasons for her to accept, she assured herself.

By the time Bryan reappeared, Amy had already retrieved plates and utensils from the cupboard. She was opening the containers of food when he joined her.

"I can stay for a few minutes," she told him, refusing to meet his gaze. "How's Dylan?"

"Not happy about missing the party in here, but resigned to his fate." A grin tugged at the corners of his mouth.

"Party" might be too strong a word, Amy speculated, as she helped herself to a small serving of rice and cashew chicken. Bryan, on the other hand, loaded up his plate.

Most of the time, Amy had no problem maintaining a conversation. She was a journalist, after all. Trained to ask questions, elicit information, put people at ease. Once again, she was forced to acknowledge that those skills deserted her around Bryan. And he seemed to be faring no better. The ticking of the clock on the wall seemed amplified in the tense quiet, and she searched in desperation for some safe topic to break the uncomfortable silence.

"Your dad went fishing, you said?" That should be innocuous enough.

"Yeah. One of his buddies has a cabin a ways down on the Cumberland. With his work schedule, Dad's never had a chance to spend much time there, but he's chomping at the bit to do more of that kind of thing now that he's retired. I'm afraid our return has messed up his plans."

Thinking of how James Healey's eyes shone when he was with his grandson, Amy shook her head. "I have a feeling he'd disagree with you. Having family close is a great blessing. I'm sure he's enjoying every minute of it."

"Still, once I get settled, I'm going to be looking for a house and arranging after-school care for Dylan. Dad has a right to his own life after all those years of a rigid work schedule. I'm sure he'll spend a lot of time with us, but I don't want him to feel obligated."

Thoughtful. Another trait she'd always admired in Bryan.

"There are a number of good day-care centers in town," Amy offered.

"Yeah."

"You don't sound too thrilled."

Shrugging, he speared a bite of chicken with his fork. "I never wanted my children raised by strangers. Neither did Darlene. She'd planned to be a stay-at-home mom. But after she—" He stopped for a second, then cleared his throat. "In the end, there wasn't any other option."

"I thought perhaps her mother watched Dylan for you."

"She helped out a couple of days a week for the first year or two. But her health was beginning to decline. It was too much for her."

The conversation Bryan had had with Kevin at the retirement party replayed in Amy's mind. Bryan had stayed in Missouri far longer than he would have liked, out of a sense of ob-

ligation to his wife's mother. Amy admired
that and was tempted to say so, but she
resisted. She'd wanted to keep the conversation light, and they'd already strayed onto
personal territory. She needed to leave before
it got any more cozy.

After one more bite of dinner, she consulted her watch, then set her fork down. "I
need to be going."

As she stood, Bryan surveyed her plate.
She'd only eaten about half of the small portion
she'd taken. "Do you want a doggie bag?"

A grin tugged at her lips. "Don't tempt me."

"There's plenty here."

"Thanks, but I had enough."

If those few mouthfuls of food comprised
a typical dinner for her, no wonder she was so
slim, Bryan thought. Maybe too slim.

"I'll just pop in and say goodbye to Dylan."

The little boy was propped up on two
pillows, paging through a picture book,
when Amy appeared in his doorway. He
greeted her with a crooked smile that tugged
at her heart.

"Are you feeling better?" She moved beside
him and sat on the edge of the bed, reaching
over to lay a gentle hand on his forehead. Still
a bit warm, but not as hot as before.

"Yeah. Maybe I could get up?" He gave her a hopeful look.

"It might be better if you rest tonight. You'll feel even better tomorrow if you do."

His face fell. "I guess."

"I'm going to go home now, but your dad will take good care of you." Out of the corner of her eye, she saw that Bryan had followed her to the room and was standing quietly at the door.

"I wish you could stay. Hey, why don't you spend the night?" His face lit up. "Could she, Dad?"

When an awkward silence followed his request, Amy stepped in, refusing to look at Bryan. "Thank you for the invitation, Dylan, but I have some things I have to do tonight."

Some of the light left his eyes. "You could come back sometime to visit, though, couldn't you?"

"We'll see."

It was an evasive answer, and from the look on his face she knew Dylan recognized it as such. Leaning over, she kissed his forehead. "I'll do my best," she whispered.

Bryan followed her back down the hall, noting that she once again checked her watch. She must have a date, he figured. It was Friday night, after all. And her social life had always been full. He waited as she reached for her purse and slung it over her shoulder, then turned back to him.

"The first order of business is a change of clothes," she told him, surveying her attire. "I don't think I want to be seen in public like this."

"I don't know. It has a certain…charm. But I suppose your date would appreciate something a bit more stylish."

Confused, she stared at him. "Date?"

He was as surprised by her response as she'd been by his comment. "I assumed that—well, it's Friday night. I mean, you're an attractive, eligible woman—" He was making a mess of this, he realized. Rather than dig himself in any deeper, he clamped his mouth shut.

He thought she had a date. A logical conclusion, she supposed. Back in their school days, she'd been a veritable social butterfly, her calendar packed full from Friday night to Sunday evening, and a lot of weeknights, as well. She should just let it pass. Let him think she had a hot date lined up. He had no interest in her, anyway. What did it matter what he thought? Let him think she was still the party girl she'd been years before.

But she *didn't* want him to think that. Even if what they'd once had was gone forever, she wanted him to know that she'd grown up and straightened out her priorities. As she searched her bag for her keys, she spoke in a conversational tone. "I don't have a date. I'm a driver for the church's meals-on-wheels program on Friday nights." When her statement drew no response, she looked over at him. *Stunned* was the only way to describe his reaction.

It took a concerted effort for Bryan to wipe the shock off his face. Then, unsure his ears had conveyed the message accurately, he asked for clarification. "You take meals to people?"

"Yes. Most of the people we serve are elderly or disabled, or struggling families. Tim's secretary, Dawn, got me involved in the program a couple of years ago."

"You don't date on Friday night?"

She sent him a direct look. "I don't date much, period."

"Why not?" The minute he asked the question, he wished he could retract it. "Sorry. That's none of my business."

Instead of responding, Amy turned and walked to the door. She had no intention of answering his question. Mostly because if she gave him an honest response, she'd have to tell him that the reason was very simple—he'd ruined her for any other man. Never once, in the ten years since they'd parted, had she found anyone to equal Bryan Healey. And she doubted she ever would. Oh, she'd tried. Any number of times. Without success. The fact that he'd moved on, given his heart to another, married and started a family—none of that mattered. Her feelings still ran as deep and strong as the Cumberland River. Yes, she'd subdued them over the years. Accepted that Bryan was lost to her. But her heart had never stopped yearning for him. And now that she'd seen the caring, loving father Bryan had matured into, her feelings were even stronger.

"Amy, I'm sorry if I offended you."

She didn't turn back. "It's okay."

No, it wasn't. He could hear the hurt in her voice, but he didn't know how to erase it. "Listen, thanks for helping with Dylan."

"No problem." She reached for the door handle, stepped across the threshold, then threw one parting remark over her shoulder. "I wouldn't have wanted to miss that story for *Nashville Living.*"

There was a time when he would have taken that comment at face value, when the undertones in her voice would have been lost to him, and he would have considered her remark one more piece of evidence that her career came first. As he looked at her now, though, across the worn oak table in his boyhood home—a table where his mother had taught him and Kevin, in her gentle way, not to judge people too harshly—he could tell from Amy's expression that she expected him to come to the very conclusion he would have arrived at a few weeks before.

Except he didn't. Since his return, he'd learned enough about the woman he'd once loved to know that she'd changed. And in other circumstances, he might even consider pursuing a relationship with her, testing the waters. But they had too much history to get past. Still, for a fleeting moment before he squelched it, the temptation to try was strong.

As Amy prepared to exit, something in Bryan's face caused her step to falter. She'd expected her words to be met with a sardonic smile. Counted on it, in fact, because that kind of reaction would help her control the regret and longing that she felt whenever she was in Bryan's presence. Instead, she had a feeling that for the first time, he'd looked past her words and into her heart, and realized that the Amy Hamilton who stood before him now had learned a whole lot since her cheerleading days. Even more, she sensed he found the changes in her appealing. Even attractive. Yet she also had the distinct impression that he was beating down that attraction with as much diligence and fear as the prairie settlers had once beaten down the dangerous brush fires that sprang up without warning in unexpected places.

Disconcerted by that realization, she turned and stepped through the door, closing it with a quiet click behind her. She understood Bryan's reluctance to consider rekindling an old romance. She, too, had reservations. There were risks, after all. A possibility that things wouldn't work out, that one or both would be hurt, just as they'd been hurt many years before. Plus, there was Dylan to consider now. She would never want to disrupt his world. Children needed stability, and his life had already been shaken up enough.

Still, as she slid behind the wheel of her car, she knew she hadn't imagined that speculative look on Bryan's face. And she allowed herself one tiny taste of something that had been long absent from her life when it came to romance.

Hope.

Chapter Nine

"Dad's taken a turn for the worse."

At Tim's ominous greeting, Amy's heart skidded to a stop, then lurched forward at double speed. She shifted the phone on her ear and tried to remain calm. "What happened?"

"Mom says he's been coughing for a couple of days, and his temperature has gone up again."

"I noticed the cough when I was there last night. Dad passed it off as allergies."

"Well, Mom thinks it's something more."

So did Amy. She still didn't like her father's color. "What's the plan?"

"Mom already called Dr. Strickland. He's ordered a chest X-ray and more blood work. Plus some other tests."

"When?"

"ASAP. I'm going to run out there and drive them to Community General now."

That news did nothing to quell Amy's alarm. If Tim was vacating his office early—even an hour early, Amy noted, checking her watch—he must be really worried. "I'll go, too."

"No need for both of us to leave work. Don't you have a press deadline coming up?"

That sounded more like Tim. "Yes."

"I'll call as soon as we know anything. Bring Heather up to speed. I'll track down Chris. Talk to you later."

The line went dead, and Amy replaced the receiver, then went in search of Heather. She dreaded passing on the latest news to her sister, who was already worried sick about their father. Although Amy planned to do her best to reassure her, she doubted whether she would succeed this time. Because she herself wasn't convinced that everything would be okay.

"Amy? Tim. Round up Heather. We need to get to the hospital right away."

Ever since Tim had driven their father to the hospital yesterday for tests, Amy had been on tenterhooks. And a visit with her father last night hadn't reassured her one iota. He'd looked pale and drawn and far weaker than he had just a couple of days before. Although she'd tried all day to concentrate on her work while they waited for the results, it had been a losing battle. The minutes had seemed like hours, the hours like weeks. By the time morning gave way to afternoon, she felt as if she'd been at work for a year. By late afternoon, she couldn't even sit at her desk anymore. She'd tried to brace herself for bad news, but she realized now that she wasn't as prepared as she'd thought. Her stomach clenched, and every nerve in her body seemed to tense in unison.

"Tell me what's going on." She tried to keep her voice calm, but a quiver ran through it.

"Mom just called from the hospital. Dad's been readmitted. Dr. Strickland is on his way from Nashville, and he wants to have a family conference."

"What's the problem?"

"I'm not sure. No one at the hospital is talking. I've already called Chris. He'll meet us there. Find Heather and meet me out front. I'll drive." The line went dead.

The short trip to the hospital was silent, as was the ride up in the elevator. Heather looked like she was about to cry, and Amy reached over to squeeze her hand as the door slid open.

But her sister was so distraught she didn't seem to notice.

When they reached Wallace's room, Chris was standing near the foot of the bed, one shoulder propped against the wall, his arms folded across his chest, his expression grim. Nora sat beside Wallace, her face almost as pale as her husband's. Amy and Heather went at once to Wallace's side, bending down to kiss his forehead, while Tim waited his turn.

"Hi, Dad." Heather's voice was tremulous.

"We came as soon as Tim called," Amy added.

Wallace shook his head. "My word, you'd think I was going down for the third time. Who's watching the store?"

Her father's attempt to lighten the atmosphere only tightened Amy's throat. "It can survive on its own for a few hours," she responded, trying to emulate his example but not quite pulling it off. As Heather moved closer and began to converse with their father, Amy stepped back. "Any news?" she asked Chris in a low voice.

"Not yet. Strickland said he'd be up as soon as he reviewed the results."

For the next half hour, the Hamiltons made a heroic effort to conduct a normal conversation.

But their collective anxiety wasn't conducive to small talk, and as the minutes ticked by, the stress level in the room inched higher and higher until it was almost as thick as the summer humidity in the Cumberland River valley. And Luke Strickland's solemn face, when he stepped into the room, did nothing to dispel it.

"Is everyone here?" As usual, he wasted no time on chitchat, but got right to the point. Amy had appreciated that straightforward approach up until now. Today, though, she almost wished he'd ease into the bad news. But her wish went unfulfilled.

"Everyone who's going to be," Tim responded.

The doctor gave a curt nod and closed the door. Despite his sometimes brusque manner, Amy was glad that her father was under his care. Luke Strickland might be young—late thirties, she estimated—but despite his age, he was the best. She was grateful he was Wallace's physician, and even more grateful that he had been willing to drive up from Nashville to deal with this crisis.

"Okay, here's what we've got," he said, his tone clinical. "Mr. Hamilton, the blood tests you had yesterday indicated that your white blood cell count is down. I had suspected that might be the case. That's why I ordered a few other tests as well. One of those revealed a fungal infection in your lungs. They aren't uncommon in bone marrow transplant patients during the first three months after surgery, but those that occur in the lungs are more worrisome because they can lead to pneumonia. We don't want to deal with that complication. That's why I want to keep you here until we get this under control. We'll begin treating you with amphotericin, which is a very powerful drug with a number of potential side effects, including headache, fever, muscle pain, fatigue and chills."

"Can't I just take this medicine at home?" Wallace asked.

"It's administered through an IV. And we need to monitor you closely while you're on it. I mentioned some of the common side effects. There are other more serious complications we'll need to watch for, as well, including cardiac irregularities, breathing difficulties, blurred vision and seizures, to name a few. We'll be drawing blood twice a day and keeping a close eye on kidney function, at least for the first two weeks you're on the drug. Does anyone have any questions?"

Too numb to respond, Amy surveyed her

siblings. They all appeared to be as shocked by the turn of events as she was. And just as unable to think of anything intelligent to ask. Other than the obvious question, of course. And no one seemed to be brave enough to voice that one. Except Nora. Despite her fragile-looking appearance, her mother had always had the courage and strength to face the truth and meet problems head-on.

"Does this infection indicate that the transplant isn't working, Doctor?" Nora's voice was calm, but anxiety stretched the skin tautly across the fine bone structure of her face as she braced herself for the response.

Dr. Strickland turned toward her mother, and there was an almost imperceptible softening in his manner. "No, Mrs. Hamilton. Not at all. The infection is a result of all the post-transplant antibiotics your husband has been taking. Those drugs are necessary to reduce the risk of bacterial infection. But they also destroy beneficial bacteria that keep fungi in check. So far, we've seen nothing to indicate that the transplant hasn't been a success. As we discussed before the surgery, however, it can take up to a year for bone marrow to function in a normal manner. That's why we need to monitor patients with great care during that period."

Her mother's relieved expression, and the doctor's clear explanation, eased Amy's mind. Although her father wasn't out of the woods, and pneumonia was a serious threat, at least the transplant wasn't failing. She felt confident that everything that could be done was being done. All she could add to the mix was prayer. And she knew her parents, Heather and Chris would be doing their part on that score as well.

"Doctor, could stress have lowered Dad's resistance? Contributed to this problem by making him more susceptible?"

From Tim's question, it was obvious he was still blaming Jeremy for Wallace's latest health crisis. But at least the doctor's reply discouraged him from that line of thought.

"Unlikely. There's a very basic medical explanation for this. Beyond that, it would be hard to establish any causal links."

Amy shot Tim a reproachful look, but he responded with a defiant lift of his chin.

"Now I would suggest that all of you go back to your normal routine and let your father get some rest. He's had a trying day." Dr. Strickland addressed this comment to the siblings.

"Thank you for making the trip from Nashville, Doctor." Nora extended her hand.

Dr. Strickland took it in both of his and gentled his voice. "And you get some rest, too, or we'll have another patient on our hands."

"He's right, Mom. I'll stay a while. You go on home," Amy offered.

"I don't want to leave your father just yet."

"At least go have something to eat," the doctor urged.

"Good idea." Tim stepped forward. "I'll take you out for dinner, Mom. Amy will stay with Dad."

Just then Ethan appeared in the doorway. Heather was beside him in an instant, and he wrapped his arms around her.

"Sorry I'm late. I didn't get your message until fifteen minutes ago," he murmured into her hair.

"Okay, Heather has a ride home." At Tim's comment, Amy shook her head. Her brother, the detail man. "Chris?" Tim continued.

"I'm officially still on patrol."

"We're set, then. Amy stays, Mom eats with me, the rest of you go back to your routine. Let's head out."

No one argued. Once Typhoon Tim was on a roll, there was no stopping him. Even Wallace didn't challenge his plan. One by one they said their goodbyes, until only Amy and her father were left. She sank into the chair beside his bed and took a deep breath.

"Tim should have been a drill sergeant," she commented.

"Takes after the old man, I guess."

"You're being too hard on yourself."

"No, I'm not. But sometimes I've been too hard on the people who worked for me. As well as my children."

At the regret in his voice, Amy wondered if he was thinking of Jeremy. She waited, but he said no more. His eyelids had drifted closed, and she was struck anew by the realization that this once powerful, tough, demanding but always fair man, who had led the Hamilton family with strength and courage, who had tackled innumerable business challenges and always emerged on top, was now facing the biggest battle of his life. Amy had always thought of her father as invincible. But as he lay spent and pale in the hospital bed, she was reminded that no one is indestructible. And as she sat beside him and watched him sleep, she prayed yet again that the Lord would see them safely through the troubles that the family now faced.

When Nora returned, Amy stood and met her at the door. "He's been sleeping since you left," she whispered.

"I'm glad. He needs the rest. You go on home, dear. You've had a couple of long days yourself."

"You should go home, too, Mom."

"I will. Tim's coming back for me in an hour or two."

"Would you like me to stay with you?"

Nora smiled. "No. You go on home. Being managing editor of *Nashville Living* is demanding, and you won't be able to do your usual stellar job if you're tired. The best thing we can do for your father now—besides pray—is make sure the business he loves doesn't falter in his absence."

Her mother was right. Conceding the point, Amy leaned over and hugged Nora. "You'll call me if you need anything, right?"

"Of course, dear. Good night."

As Amy emerged from the elevator into the lobby a few minutes later, she noted that the autumn evening was pitch-dark already. Winter would be upon them before they knew it. There was even a slight chill in the air, producing a tingle that warned of cooler air soon to follow, she realized, as she stepped outside. Later tonight, it would get quite a bit colder. But right now, the fresh, clean air was invigorating after the antiseptic hospital smell that they'd become all too familiar with over the past few months. She walked toward the parking lot, inhaling deep, cleansing breaths, as if…

All at once her step faltered, and then she came to an abrupt stop. What on earth had she been thinking? She didn't have her car! In all the excitement, it seemed no one, including her, had remembered that she'd gotten a ride with Tim.

Dismayed, Amy planted her hands on her hips and considered her options. She could call one of her siblings. But Chris was still working, Heather was with Ethan, and Tim was no doubt back at the office trying to catch up on the work he'd missed in the past couple of days. She could call a cab, she supposed. But it might take a while for one to arrive. Or she could walk. Her fashionable pumps with their slender three-inch heels weren't exactly designed for long-distance hiking, but it wasn't all that far to The Enclave. Besides, a walk might clear her head, help her relax, she decided, striking out.

The first few blocks were no problem; in fact, she enjoyed herself. Just as she'd hoped, the fresh air worked wonders. She'd been depressed when she'd left the hospital, but her attitude improved with every step and every breath. Until her feet started to protest.

By the time she reached Sugar Tree Park, just a few blocks from home, she was almost limping. She headed toward the first bench she saw and sank onto it, reaching down to ease off one shoe and massage her foot. If a cab appeared, she decided she'd flag it down, despite the short remaining distance. Even another block was more than she could face in these shoes.

As Amy turned her attention to her other foot, she recalled Nora telling them as children that there was a price for vanity. Amy didn't think she'd been talking about footwear, but the axiom fit, nonetheless. One of her first orders of business when life slowed down—*if* it ever slowed down—was to buy some sensible shoes, she resolved.

In the meantime, she'd manage to get home, her protesting feet notwithstanding. Only not just yet. She'd give herself ten minutes first, even though she knew that brief rest wasn't going to make the final few blocks any easier to traverse.

The woman seated on the park bench was in shadows for the most part, but something about her posture caught Bryan's attention. It wasn't only the slumped, weary lines of her body that caused him to take a second look. It was just that she seemed…familiar.

As he drew closer, Bryan slowed his car and squinted at the dim figure. Just then, she raised her head, and her blond hair glinted in the street-light. It was Amy! What in the world was she doing sitting in Sugar Tree Park at—he checked the digital clock that glowed on his dashboard—seven-thirty at night, holding her shoe?

A wave of concern washed over him. Although the light was far too dim to read her expression, he had a feeling that if he could look into her eyes, he'd see discouragement and fatigue in their depths. That shouldn't surprise him, he supposed, given all the problems in the Hamilton family. But it still didn't explain why she was here in the dark alone on a cool fall evening…still in her work clothes, he realized. Unless something else had happened.

Her personal affairs weren't any of his business, of course. Maybe she'd just needed some time by herself. And she was only a few blocks from The Enclave. She could be home in a matter of minutes. Still, for safety reasons alone he didn't like the fact that she was sitting in a deserted park in the dark. Davis Landing had a very low crime rate, but it wasn't utopia.

Bad things did happen on occasion. And he didn't want one of them to happen to Amy.

As he debated how best to proceed, she slipped her shoe back on and stood. Perhaps the thing to do was follow her home, at a safe distance. That way he wouldn't intrude, but he could assure himself that she arrived there without incident. Yes, he decided, that was a good plan.

At least it was—until she started to walk and he noticed that she seemed to be limping.

Trashing his original plan, Bryan put the car in gear, made a U-turn and pulled up alongside her, easing his window down as he came to a stop. "Amy?"

Her step slowed and she peered into the dim interior of the car. At the sight of Bryan's face, she almost wept with relief. They might not be on the best of terms, but surely he'd give her a ride home.

As if reading her mind, he reached across and pushed open the passenger door. "You look like you could use a lift."

Without hesitation, Amy stepped off the curb. "I think I know how the Israelites felt when they came upon the manna from heaven," she told him as she slid onto the seat and summoned up a weary smile.

An answering smile tugged at the corners of his mouth. "I don't think I've ever been compared to manna before."

"Trust me, it's a compliment. You saved my life. I wasn't sure I was going to make it to The Enclave."

He eyed her sling-back pumps with their high, slender heels. "Walking home from work in those kind of shoes probably isn't the best idea."

"I wasn't coming from work. I've been at Community General."

"You walked all the way from Community General?" He turned to stare at her.

"It's not that far."

"It is in those shoes."

She couldn't argue with that. "I guess I wasn't thinking too clearly."

"Is everything all right?"

"No. Dad was readmitted today." All at once her voice was soft and uncertain.

"Problems with the transplant?"

"No. But he's developed a fungal infection in his lungs. According to his doctor, the antibiotics that kill the bad bacteria also kill the good ones that ward off infections like this. He's worried this might lead to pneumonia."

"I'm sorry." He didn't know what else to

say. Medical problems and complications were all too familiar to him, and he'd done more than his share of time in hospitals. It was gut-wrenching, emotionally draining and totally disruptive. As a result of his experiences, Bryan had developed a very healthy appreciation for normal, everyday routine. Something that had been absent from Amy's life for at least the past few months, he suspected.

"Thanks. Dad's illness has been hard on everyone. Not to mention all of the other problems we've had to deal with."

He darted another quick look in her direction. He'd noticed the faint blue smudges under her eyes when he'd first come back to Davis Landing, but they were even more prominent now. And he recognized them for what they were: visible evidence of stress and sleepless nights. His own face had looked like that on more than one occasion. Often for weeks at a time. He also knew that the invisible evidence was even more distressing. Taut nerves, knots in your stomach, grinding teeth. Yeah, he'd been there.

"What brings you to Davis Landing at night?"

Her question pulled him back to the present. "I had to drop Dylan off at a friend's house for a sleepover. His first. I don't know who was more anxious about it—him or me. I ended up sitting across the street in my car for half an hour before I could force myself to drive away."

A brief smile flitted across her face. "He'll do fine. He strikes me as a very bright, capable little boy."

"He is."

They were approaching The Enclave, and Amy turned to Bryan. "I appreciate the ride. I tried to focus on having dinner instead of thinking about my feet, but it wasn't working. You came along at just the right time."

Her last comment jarred him a bit, though he knew she'd been referring to tonight, not his return to Davis Landing. Still, it seemed heavy with meaning. However, he chose to zero in on her other remark. "You haven't had dinner yet?"

"No."

"I haven't, either."

Surprised, she turned to him. It was difficult to read his face in the dim light, but his response had seemed to suggest they eat together. And perhaps she owed him that, since he'd come to her rescue. "I don't have a lot in the refrigerator, but I'm sure I could scrounge up something if you'd like to join me." Her voice was tentative.

Now it was Bryan's turn to be surprised. He wasn't sure why he'd thrown out that comment about dinner, and in retrospect he realized it had sounded like he was angling for an invitation. And perhaps he had been. Not on a conscious level, of course. He was sure of that. But perhaps his subconscious had prompted the remark, inspired by a subliminal urge to learn more about the woman she had become.

Already he'd learned a great deal, enough to intrigue him. He'd observed Amy's considerate and empathetic interactions with staff members, family and friends. He'd found out about her involvement with the meals-on-wheels program. He'd watched her handle, with grace and compassion, the problems that plagued her family. He'd come to recognize the important role that her renewed faith played in her life. In other words, he'd learned enough to realize that if it wasn't for the history between them, he might consider pursuing a relationship with this woman, who had stolen his heart so many years before. Yet even that obstacle seemed to be diminishing in importance as time went by.

In fact, if he was honest with himself, Bryan *wanted* to spend the evening with Amy. He was tired of second-guessing his feelings for her, tired of the caution sign that flashed every time they were together, tired of ignoring the thaw that was taking place in his heart. Tired enough to decide that for once he was just going to follow his instincts. And tired enough to ignore the little voice in the back of his mind, which reminded him that doing so could change the course of their relationship forever.

Taking a deep breath, he tried for a conversational tone. And almost pulled it off. "After the day you've had, I don't expect you to fix me dinner. How about I order us some pizza?"

Chapter Ten

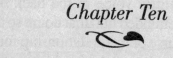

Although Amy knew there was little hope that things could ever be put right between them, she couldn't stop the warm rush of pleasure that washed over her at the thought of spending an hour or two with Bryan. In a day fraught with worry, his offer was the one bright spot. "That would be nice," she accepted.

After directing him to a parking spot, Amy led the way into the lobby.

"Evening, Amy," the security guard greeted her.

"Hi, Russ." She didn't stop to chat. The smile she'd pasted on her face couldn't quite mask the grimace of pain underneath, and Bryan knew that every step she took was agony.

He had time for no more than a fleeting impression of the tasteful lobby of The Enclave before they stepped into the elevator. Amy depressed the button with the *four* on it, and as the door slid shut she balanced herself against the wall with one hand, reaching down with the other one to slip off her shoes. "Sorry. I can't stand these another second."

In heels, Amy was only a couple of inches shorter than him. Now the gap widened to five or six inches. She felt small beside him, and somehow vulnerable. In the office, she came across as assertive and strong and in control. Those were qualities Bryan admired. He'd always liked women who had the confidence to step in and take charge. Now, away from the public eye, in her stocking feet, her shoulders sagging under her burden of worry, he had a completely different impression of her. Yet it was just as appealing. Although Amy was the kind of woman who would want the man in her life to hold her hand, not hold her up, he had the feeling that there were times, like tonight, when she might welcome a sympathetic shoulder to cry on—in a figurative sense, of course.

They'd paused in front of a door, and Amy inserted a key, then pushed it open. She flipped on a switch as they entered, and warm, golden light bathed the room. "Make yourself comfortable. I'm ditching the shoes. And if you don't mind, I'm going to change into something a little more comfortable."

"Take your time."

She disappeared down a small hall, and he noted that there were only two doors opening off it. A bedroom and a bath, no doubt. The rest of the unit seemed to consist of a spacious living room that opened through an archway into a small dining area, and a compact but well-equipped kitchen.

As he strolled around, he revised his image of The Enclave. While some of the units might be quite elaborate, Amy's wasn't. The clean, simple architectural lines were enhanced by tasteful, understated furnishings. A sofa, covered in cream-colored damask, faced the fireplace, which was framed by a brass screen. A side chair in cobalt-blue was angled toward the couch, and emerald-green throw pillows added bright spots of color. So did a soft throw, in a Monet-like pattern, that was draped over the sofa. A crystal bowl filled with foil-wrapped Hershey's kisses was the sole ornamentation on the glass-topped coffee table. Several large green plants, including a robust ficus tree, were arrayed on the dove-gray carpeting and warmed up the space. The room was elegant and soothing, though by no means pretentious or ostentatious. It was, in a word, classy. Just like the woman.

By the time Amy reappeared, in jeans that hugged her trim hips and a soft-looking V-neck sweater the exact color of her eyes, Bryan had ordered the pizza and set the table. She had on a pair of fuzzy, well-worn slippers, and he grinned when he saw them. "You do look more comfortable."

"Much."

"I ordered a pepperoni and sausage with everything except olives. Is that all right?"

Just like old times, Amy thought with a wistful pang. He even remembered her aversion to olives. "Great. Thanks."

Now that they were in better light, Bryan was struck anew by the deep weariness in her face. And by the strain. He could see it in the tense line of her jaw, the tautness of her skin, the stiffness of her lips. That's what long-term stress did to you. That, and other, less visible, things. He wondered how long it had been since she'd truly relaxed.

"Would you like some soda?" She tossed the question over her shoulder as she headed toward the kitchen.

"Yeah. That would be fine. Although, to be

honest, you look like you could use something stronger."

She reached into the refrigerator and withdrew two Cokes. "Thanks a lot. That's just what my ego needs after the day I've had." Her words were softened by her teasing tone.

"I'm serious. Maybe a glass of wine would help you unwind."

"It might, if I drank. Though this would be the time to start, if I was so inclined, with all that's been going on."

Memories of the frat party flitted across Bryan's mind, and he sent her a puzzled look. He'd followed her to the kitchen, and now he folded his arms across his chest and propped a shoulder against the door frame. "You don't drink?"

She angled a look at him, knowing what he was remembering. "Not for a long time."

More evidence she'd changed, Bryan thought. Then a smile whispered at the corners of his mouth. "But you haven't given up *all* your vices."

Curious, she stared at him. "What do you mean?"

"I saw the Hershey's kisses." They'd been one of her favorite treats in high school. Almost an addiction.

Soft color warmed her face. "Guilty as charged. That's a love affair that will never end." As soon as she said the words, she regretted them. They were innocuous enough in the context she'd used them, but not the wisest choice considering her history with Bryan. And he must have felt the same, since silence greeted her comment. Fortunately, the phone rang just then and dispelled the awkward moment. Relieved, she reached for it. "Must be our pizza." She listened for a second, then spoke. "Thanks, Russ. We'll be right down."

"I'll go," Bryan offered, already heading for the door. "Why don't you sit down and rest your feet?"

"But I invited you. This is my treat."

"Not this time." He was out the door before she could protest. Not that she was inclined to. Her feet were killing her. That would teach her to attempt a marathon walk in high heels, she thought, as she gingerly moved over to the small cherry table and sank onto the cushioned seat of one of the matching chairs.

Bryan was back in no time, and enticing aromas wafted toward her as he carried in the box and set it on the table.

"This smells great!" She pried open the lid, then reached for a large slice. Bryan followed her example, and for the next few minutes conversation lagged as they focused on eating.

When they'd both taken the edge off their hunger, Amy leaned back and slowed her pace. "I haven't had pizza since your welcoming party at work. It's one of those things that—" She stopped mid-sentence as a blob of tomato sauce fell smack onto the middle of her sweater. This was getting to be a pattern, she realized. First, her white top at James's retirement party. Then her linen jacket when Dylan was sick. Now tomato sauce. Bryan was going to think she was a klutz. "I'll get some napkins," she said, starting to rise.

A hand on her arm restrained her. "Stay put. Where are they?"

"In the kitchen. Bottom shelf of the cabinet next to the microwave."

Bryan located them with no problem, grabbed a handful and returned to the dining room. As he set them on the table, something fluttered to the floor, and he reached down to retrieve it, realizing it was a check. For a sizable amount. Signed by Amy and made out to Youth Connections, a sports program targeted to at-risk kids. He'd read about it in the church bulletin.

Touched by her generosity, yet feeling that he'd somehow violated her privacy, he set it on the table without comment. Amy flicked a glance toward it as she dabbed at the stain, and her hand faltered. She kept her charitable activities low-key, the sense of satisfaction she received from being able to help those less fortunate all the reward she needed or wanted. Public accolades held no appeal. Even her family wasn't privy to the extent of her generosity. Chris was aware of her support of Youth Connections, of course, since he was one of the cofounders and was involved in running the organization. But no one else knew. Until now.

Sensing her embarrassment, Bryan felt obliged to say something. "Sorry. It must have been in with the napkins."

Lifting one shoulder, she went back to work on her sweater. "I forgot I put it in there. I've been a little distracted lately. Well, I think I got as much of this out as I'm going to be able to without—" All at once her eyes widened, and she jumped up. "Ow! Oh, that hurts!" she muttered, limping around in a circle, her face contorted in pain.

Alarmed, Bryan vaulted to his feet as well, almost choking on the piece of pizza he was chewing. "What's wrong?" he asked between coughs.

"Muscle spasm. Happens sometimes when I'm on my feet too long in high heels." She tried to put her weight on her foot and winced. "Those shoes are history tomorrow," she declared through clenched teeth, hobbling into the living room.

Wiping his mouth on a napkin, Bryan came up behind her and took her arm, leading her to the couch. "Sit down. I think I can help."

"Sitting doesn't work. I have to put weight on it. Ouch!" Her whole body went rigid as another spasm twisted her foot.

"Look, give this a try, okay?" He eased her down, angling her body toward him, then sat beside her. "Which foot?"

"Right."

He pulled her feet onto his lap and pulled off her right slipper. "Where does it hurt?"

"The bottom. Near the middle and…right there!" His fingers had found the spot.

"Okay, try to relax."

"Yeah, right." She hated these spasms. She got them once in while after a long day in heels, or when her stress level was elevated. Considering both were true today, it was no wonder her feet had rebelled.

Instead of responding, Bryan went to work, his hands firm and sure, feeling out the muscles that were bunched into a hard knot and then massaging them with even, rhythmic strokes, exerting just the right amount of pressure.

After a few minutes, Amy began to relax. "Wow! Where did you learn to do that?"

"I've had some practice."

At his careful, noncommittal response, she suspected that his practice had been with Darlene. Well, whatever. It had been a godsend for her tonight.

When her right foot lay relaxed in his hands, he reached for her left foot.

"That one's okay," she told him.

"Right now. But it might give you problems later."

That was true. Often, just when she got one foot to settle down, the other went ballistic. "Okay, Doctor Healey."

Her teasing tone brought the flicker of a smile to his lips.

Long after the spasms had been banished, Bryan continued his ministrations. Amy didn't object. In fact, she wished they would go on forever. His hands on her bare feet felt wonderful. More relaxed than she had been in months, she let her head drop to the back of the sofa. Her eyelids drifted close, and in seconds she was asleep.

When Bryan looked over at her a few minutes later, the tranquil lines of her face and her even breathing told him she'd succumbed to exhaustion. And that it was time for him to go.

But he didn't want to leave. Being with her like this reminded him of all the good times they'd had, the closeness they'd shared. An unexpected yearning swept over him, a wish that they could revisit or recreate those times. And for a fleeting moment, he not only wondered if that was possible, but believed that it might be.

The question was, did he even want to make the attempt? Or, more importantly, *should* he make the attempt? Wouldn't it somehow dishonor the memory of Darlene, and the quiet, deep love they had shared?

Bryan wasn't sure. And tonight, when Amy seemed vulnerable and he suddenly felt more alone than he had in a very long time, wasn't the time to find out. It would be better if he left. Now.

Hoping to slip out without disturbing her, he eased her feet off his lap and started to stand. As he rose, she stirred and looked up at him, blinking.

"Did I fall asleep?" she mumbled.

"Out like a light."

Swinging her feet to the floor, she rubbed her eyes with the backs of her hands, in an endearing gesture that tugged at his heart and reminded him of the way Dylan awakened. "Sorry."

"You seemed like you needed the rest."

Standing, she tested her feet, and a sleepy smile lifted her lips. "All gone. You must have magic hands."

"Nope. Just a lot of practice. Darlene liked foot rubs when she was pregnant." He wasn't sure why he'd mentioned his wife. Maybe to remind him to keep his distance from this appealing woman until he'd worked through his issues. Maybe to warn her off. Whatever the motivation, it seemed to have worked. Amy's smile faded a bit at the edges, like an old photograph.

"Lucky woman," she said.

"I can let myself out."

"I'll walk you to the door."

She followed him in silence, then stood on the threshold, leaning against the edge of the open door as he turned to her.

"Get some rest."

"Thanks to you, I think I will. I appreciate everything you did tonight, Bryan. The ride, the pizza, the foot massage. I'm used to managing things on my own, but…well…it's been tough for the past few months, and it felt…nice…to have someone help out."

For the first time since his return, Bryan realized that behind the independent face Amy turned to the world lay a deep loneliness. Although she'd always been close to her family, they were otherwise occupied. Her father was sick. Her mother was preoccupied with her husband's health. Her siblings were busy with their own lives. Heather was engaged, and Chris was close to proposing, if the rumors at work were to be believed. His impression of Tim could be summed up in one word: workaholic; the second-oldest brother seemed to have little time for anything but his job. Jeremy and Melissa were gone. Which meant that, by and large, Amy was alone. Even more alone than he was. At least he had Dylan, and his father was always available for conversation or advice, or to help with his grandson.

Startled by this insight, Bryan stared at the woman across from him. In many ways, she was the same girl he remembered from years before. Her physical features hadn't changed all that much. But there was a maturity about her that had never been there before, a sense of direction and purpose, an impression that she'd found her place in the world and was at peace with it. In other words, she'd grown up. And, in the process, become even more appealing.

All at once, Bryan yearned to pull her close, to comfort her, to hold her until she felt strong again. Yet he knew that the impulse was driven by more than altruism and compassion. He also wanted to kiss her, to taste the sweet lips he remembered with a sudden, surprisingly vivid intensity from years before, to bury his hands in her silky hair, to hold her in his arms and forget about the past and the future and focus only on now, this moment.

As he looked at her, her eyes grew luminous, almost as if she knew what he was thinking—and that she felt the same way. Without conscious decision, he reached up and brushed some of the silky strands of golden hair back from her face. Her lips parted slightly at his touch, in invitation, and he swayed toward her. She lifted her face and leaned in. He dropped his chin and...

The elevator door slid open, and a laughing couple emerged. Bryan snapped back and dropped his hand. Amy blinked once, then twice, before she lowered her head and took a deep breath.

Bryan waited until the couple had passed before he spoke. "I—I'd better be going." His voice came out in a hoarse rasp.

"Yeah. Thanks again." Her own voice sounded shaky, and she didn't raise her head. But the grip she had on the edge of the door had turned her knuckles white.

"I'll see you at work."

"Right."

As Bryan turned and walked down the hall, trying to rein in his galloping pulse, he heard her door shut with a soft click behind him. Equal parts regret and relief washed over him. In another few seconds, he'd have claimed her sweet lips. And moved them into brand-new territory that was fraught with danger and uncertainties. Maybe they were destined to go there. More and more, he was beginning to think they were. But he wasn't sure this was the time. Not yet.

As he rode down in the silent elevator and exited into the cool night, he glanced up at the stars. In recent weeks, since he'd resumed weekly church attendance and started listening—really listening—to the minister's words, he'd begun to find his way back to

God, to let go of the anger in his heart for the losses he'd sustained and open it to the healing love of the Lord. And he'd been inspired by Amy's faith, which had remained staunch even in the face of all that had beset the Hamilton family.

His once-strong faith still needed bolstering, however. And his prayer life hadn't returned to the conversational level he'd enjoyed years before. He was trying, though. Especially when he needed guidance. And there was no question that tonight fell into that category. So as he walked to his car in the dark parking lot, he sent a silent prayer heavenward.

Lord, please guide me as I try to discern the path You desire for me. Give me the wisdom to know Your will and the courage to follow it. Forgive me for all the bitterness and anger I've held in my heart. Help me to let it go once and for all. Because I know now that until I do, I'll never be able to claim the future You desire for me. And help me make peace with the past that Amy and I share, and to trust that as I travel the road ahead, You will be beside me. Wherever it may lead.

Chapter Eleven

"Hey, Dad, do you think Amy will be here today?" Dylan scanned the perimeter of the lake in Sugar Tree Park as he spoke.

Setting the boat on the placid water, Bryan handed his son the remote control. "I don't know, champ. She's a busy lady."

"I saw her at church this morning. I waved at her, but she didn't wave back. Maybe she doesn't like me anymore." Dylan hung his head and scuffed the toe of his shoe in the damp earth.

With a pang, Bryan dropped down onto the balls of his feet and placed a hand on the little boy's shoulder. "Of course she likes you. She told me that herself. But her dad is pretty sick, so she has a lot on her mind. When people are worried, or when they're sad, sometimes they don't notice things. I'm sure she didn't even see you waving at her."

"You think so?"

"Uh-huh."

"I like her a lot, Dad."

"I know."

"Do you like her, too?"

With his son's frank, guileless green eyes staring straight into his just inches away, it was hard to be anything but honest. "Yeah. I like her."

"A lot?"

Deciding that evasive maneuvers were called for, Bryan tried a non-answer. "She's a nice lady." Then he changed the subject, hoping to distract his son. "Let's see if you remember how to work those controls."

The tactic didn't work.

"Remember that day she came to my school and that man took pictures? She told me she liked kids, but that she didn't have any of her own. Did you know that?"

"Yes. She's not married, Dylan. Only people who have been married have children." Or should have, he modified in silence.

"You mean she's all by herself?"

Thinking back two nights, when he'd driven her home and realized that she was far more alone than he'd ever imagined, he wasn't quite sure how to answer Dylan's question. "Well, she has a mom and dad and brothers and sisters."

"Do they all live together? Like me and you and Grandpa?"

"No. Amy lives in a condo."

"And nobody lives there with her?"

"No."

"I bet she's lonesome."

Bryan was beginning to suspect the same thing. But his spoken words were different. "She's very busy with her job, Dylan. She doesn't have time to get lonesome."

"But what about at night?" His son was nothing if not persistent. "Like when you come home from work. There's me and Grandpa to keep you company, and we all eat dinner together. Who does Amy eat with?"

Good question. No one, most likely. And Bryan knew firsthand that eating solitary meals was one of the loneliest activities in the world. Food was meant to be shared over laughter and love and conversation. That's how it had been for him growing up, and during his marriage. He couldn't imagine choosing to live any other way.

Yet that seemed to be Amy's lifestyle. Whether by choice or circumstance, he wasn't quite sure anymore. When he'd first arrived back in town, he'd assumed she was single because she hadn't had time for romance and love, that work was the focus of her life. Since then, he'd been forced to revise that opinion. Yes, her career was important to her. It was a priority. But if he was a betting man, he'd wager that it wasn't the only priority. Or maybe even the most important one. That somewhere along the way she'd found perspective. Yet if that was the case, why wasn't she married? And why hadn't she started a family of her own? She was a beautiful, intelligent woman. He'd seen how well she interacted with Dylan, sensed that she'd be a wonderful mother. But still, there was no husband, no child, in her life. Why?

"Dad?" Dylan tugged at his sleeve and repeated the question. "Who does Amy eat with?"

"I don't know. No one, I guess."

"Maybe she could eat with us sometime."

"Maybe."

"How about tonight, Dad? We could call her. Grandpa wouldn't mind."

"Not tonight, champ. It's not polite to invite people at the last minute."

Dylan's face fell and he looked down again.

"I wish she could come. I know she isn't my mom, but…well, when I'm with her it kind of seems like she is." He lifted his head and looked at Bryan. "I like that, Dad. It makes me feel good. You know?"

As a matter of fact, he did. The more he was around Amy, the more *he* liked the feeling, too. But he wasn't ready to deal with that. Not yet. Reaching over, he ruffled Dylan's hair. "I know. And we'll see her again soon. At church next Sunday, for sure. Maybe even before that. Now, let's do some sailing."

Once he refocused Dylan's attention, it took only a couple of minutes for the boy to become absorbed in his game. To put aside the earlier conversation and forget about Amy and her appealing qualities and her solitary meals and her worries and her loneliness.

Bryan wished he could be so easily distracted. But he didn't have his son's mental dexterity. She was on his mind more and more, with the result that he found it less and less easy to concentrate on anything else. The time was coming when he'd have to deal with his growing feelings for her and to reconcile them with his love for Darlene, though he wasn't quite sure how to go about that.

But as he watched Dylan sail his boat, an idea came to him. One he decided to pursue later that evening.

From his seat on the wooden bench, Bryan had a nice view down the sloping lawn of the church to the river below and the skyline of Davis Landing on the other side. Although *skyline* was a pretty ambitious description, considering that most of the buildings were only three or four stories tall. Just a few rose higher, including The Enclave, one of the tallest buildings in town.

As he looked at it, Bryan wondered what Amy was doing. Was she there, or at the hospital? As Dylan had noticed, she'd seemed preoccupied in church this morning. Although he'd been concerned that their next meeting would be awkward as a result of their near-kiss Thursday night, his apprehension had been needless. He'd managed to avoid her all day at work Friday, and she hadn't even acknowledged his presence in church. She and Heather and Chris had sat in a protective huddle around their mother, and none of the Hamiltons had appeared to be present at the service in anything more than body. Then again, maybe they had just been deep in conversation with the Lord. That's what the house of God was for, after all. And that was the reason he'd come here after eating dinner with his father and Dylan.

Bryan hadn't been surprised to find that the church had been locked after the six o'clock service. But as he'd settled on the nearby bench, he'd consoled himself with the fact that at least he was close to God's house. Not that proximity to a physical structure was necessary in order to talk with the Lord, of course. Still, he'd thought it might be easier here. However, after twenty minutes of contemplation he was no closer to figuring out what he should do than he'd been when he'd first sat down. He still felt restless and unsettled and uncertain.

"Bryan? I thought that was you. Nice to see you."

Turning, Bryan saw Pastor Abernathy approaching. They'd chatted a time or two, and Bryan had found the man to be empathetic and insightful. He seemed like a straight shooter, too, and each time Bryan encountered him his estimation of the minister grew.

"Hello, Pastor. I hope you don't mind that I borrowed your bench."

"It belongs to all the faithful. And I'm glad it's being put to use. Mind if I join you for a minute?"

"Not at all." Bryan scooted over, and the man sat beside him.

Pastor Abernathy looked out over the river and drew a contented breath. "I sit here myself quite a lot. I like to watch the river flowing by, steady and sure and placid. It reminds me that even amidst turmoil, some things can be counted on. Like this river. And our faith. Knowing that there are certainties like that in life brings a sense of peace and hope that eases the mind."

Although he hadn't thought of it in quite that way, Bryan liked the analogy, even if the setting hadn't worked the same magic for him as it seemed to for the pastor. He wondered how honest he should be.

"I like that thought." He chose his words with care, trying to gauge the man's reactions as he spoke. "But to be honest, I'm afraid neither the river nor my faith has given me much peace of mind lately."

To Bryan's relief, there was no recrimination on the man's face. Only a quiet empathy, an invitation, almost, to share more. Yet he didn't push. He just opened the door.

"Life can shake even the firmest faith," he noted in a quiet voice. "Your father told me a little bit about your loss. And Dylan's health problems. I'm very sorry."

Turning away, Bryan looked out over the river. The setting sun was gilding the ribbon of blue and burnishing the gold-and-red autumn leaves on the hills through which it wound. If Darlene had been here, she would have reveled in this display of God's handiwork, he reflected. Thanks to her, he'd learned to notice—and appreciate—such moments of beauty.

"My wife would have enjoyed this view." Bryan's voice was soft, and his eyes warmed as he thought about the quiet, constant love they'd shared. "And thanks to her, I'm enjoying it, too. She opened my eyes to a lot of things."

"Then she gave you a great and lasting gift."

"She gave me many gifts, including a wonderful son and a second chance at love. She taught me the true meaning of selflessness. And she brought a sweetness to my life, a fullness, that made me feel richer than any millionaire." His voice choked on the last word, and he cleared his throat.

"Those things are a priceless legacy. Yet

because she gave you so much, I'm sure her death is even harder to bear."

At the minister's gentle, understanding tone, Bryan turned back to him. "It is. When she first died, I grieved with an intensity I didn't think possible. And I raged against a God who'd taken away the woman I loved and left me alone to cope with a tiny infant who was fighting for his own life." Bryan raked his fingers through his hair, his face desolate. "I'd always thought I had a strong faith, but when it was tested I realized that it wasn't all that solid after all. I felt as if God had deserted me, and without that anchor I was like a boat set adrift on the Cumberland—out of control, at the mercy of the currents, with no way to protect myself from the debris that swept past or the obstacles that loomed ahead."

"And how do you feel now, Bryan?"

"Better, I guess. I started attending church again when I came home, and your sermons have helped steer me back on the right path. They've been a great comfort."

"I'm glad of that. But I'm only the messenger. The real source of comfort is my Boss." He flashed his visitor a grin, and Bryan's own lips turned up in response. "It sounds like you're finding your way back to the Lord, and that's a great blessing. But I sense you're still troubled about something."

The man was perceptive, no question about it. Bryan rested his forearms on his thighs and stared at his hands as he clasped them between his knees. "I am. You know the Hamiltons, of course."

"They're in my prayers daily. This has been a time of great trial for them."

"Well, the reason I'm troubled is related to one of them." As briefly as he could, Bryan explained his connection to Amy, their parting years before, and his growing feelings for her. "The thing is, I think perhaps the Lord brought me home for a reason. That maybe we were meant to have that interlude apart, but now the time has come for us to be together. Yet I have this sense that if I return to the woman I first chose as my wife, I'll somehow be dishonoring the love that Darlene and I shared."

As he reflected on that, Pastor Abernathy's face grew thoughtful. "I understand your concern, Bryan. Yet many years have passed since you first loved Amy Hamilton. Would you say that the two of you are the same people you were ten or twelve years ago?"

Bryan considered the question. "No. We've both done a lot of growing up."

"What you're telling me, then, is that you've fallen in love with the woman Amy has become, not the girl she was."

He gave a slow nod. "Yes."

"Do you think she feels the same way?"

Recalling the look in her eyes Thursday night when he'd almost kissed her, and the emotion he'd seen in their depths on more than one occasion, that answer, too, seemed clear. "Yes."

The man laid a hand on Bryan's shoulder. "I admire your desire to honor the love you and your wife shared. But if you want my opinion, I don't see how falling in love again will violate that. Whether it's with the woman Amy has become or some other woman. The heart has a great capacity to love. An endless capacity, in fact. Loving someone new doesn't change the love you give, or have given, to others. That will always be uniquely theirs. It just means that you've decided to tap into the reservoir of love that hasn't yet been used."

Rising, he rested one hand on the back of the bench and looked at Bryan. "I spent some time in Vermont, and I like to compare love to maple syrup. Each year, the maple trees are tapped. By the next year, the supply of sap has been replenished and they have more to give.

Love is like that, too. There's always more, welling up inside, if we just reach down deep enough and release it. But the sap in maple syrup is only the raw material. After it's been released, it has to be boiled—tested by fire. Then it's filtered until all the impurities are removed. The work isn't easy. It can be a hard, messy job. But in the process, the sap becomes sweeter and reaches its full potential. Just like a love that weathers adversity."

Pastor Abernathy's face grew earnest and intent, much like it did when he spoke from the pulpit. "The thing is, that process of refinement can—and should—be a job every one of us tackles in all our relationships. Perhaps never with more diligence than in the kind of love that ultimately leads to the exchange of vows that unites a man and woman as one flesh. And even though many of us only take on that job once in our lives, there's no rule that says you can't have a second chance. We just need to listen to our hearts and trust that the Lord will guide us in right paths if that opportunity comes along."

When he finished, a smile chased away the serious look on his face. "Well, now. I didn't intend to preach twice today."

"I'm glad you did." Although the minister's

analogy had been folksy, Bryan had been touched by the deeper meaning. "It gave me food for thought. And speaking of food…" He consulted his watch. "Dylan and my dad are waiting until I come back to have dessert. I'm sure Dylan is chomping at the bit, since we're having brownies with ice cream." He rose and held out his hand. "Thank you."

The man took it in a firm clasp. "Like I said, I'm just the messenger. And I'm always available as a sounding board. Now go enjoy your dessert."

As Bryan set off across the lawn toward his car, his mind was whirling. In the space of a few minutes, Pastor Abernathy had helped him get a better handle on his issues than all the weeks of solo soul searching he'd done. Even though the road ahead was still a bit hazy, the fog was starting to lift. And as the view began to clear, one word from the minister's maple syrup analogy stuck in his mind.

Sap.

Because he was beginning to believe that's just what he'd be if he let Amy slip through his fingers again.

"Have you seen this morning's *Observer*?" Amy gulped down the rest of her orange juice, reached for her briefcase and checked her watch. "No, Tim. It's only seven in the morning. I usually don't read it until I get to the office."

"You'd better look now. Page five. And sit down first."

At his grim tone, Amy's fingers tightened around the phone. "Okay. Hang on." Setting the phone down, she dug through her briefcase and pulled out the *Dispatch*'s rival paper, which was delivered to her door every morning. As her father always said, it was important to know what the competition was up to.

Bracing herself, she opened the folded paper to page five and scanned the headlines. It didn't take her long to find the one Tim had referred to, topping the daily feature "The Gossip Guru." She read it once. Then read it again.

There was only one adjective that came close to capturing her reaction.

Horrified.

There, in bold type, the *Observer* had offered the latest morsel in what had fast gone from friendly rivalry to a seeming vendetta against the Hamilton family: Media Mogul's Love Child?

Sorry now that she hadn't taken Tim's advice, Amy sank onto a stool at the island in her kitchen as she scanned the insinuation-laden lead item in the column, feeling sicker by the minute. "Has Mom seen this yet?"

"I hope not. I'm on my way there now. I'm calling from my cell. See if you can catch Heather before she leaves for the office. I'll track down Chris. I think we need to meet at the house and talk with Mom about how to handle this."

"Okay. We'll see you there."

Just as Amy was heading out the door, an emergency phone call from the office delayed her several minutes. When she finally pulled up in front of the Hamilton home half an hour later, Chris's patrol car, Heather's deep blue Saab and Tim's silver BMW were already spaced along the circular driveway. Double-parking next to Tim's car, she took the front steps two at a time and pushed open the door. A subdued murmur of voices from the back parlor guided her footsteps, and seconds later she stepped into the casual room where the family had always relaxed together.

Her mother was perched on the edge of a comfortable upholstered chair, and one look at her pinched face heightened Amy's fear that the *Observer*'s latest installment might do her in. Conversation stopped as she crossed the room and embraced the older woman in a tight hug. When she finally released her mother and backed up, Nora managed to dredge up a smile and give her oldest daughter's arm a reassuring squeeze.

"Everything will be fine," she said, directing her comment first to Amy, then turning to encompass her other children when she continued. "As I already told the rest of you, I have absolutely no doubt that your father has been true to me since the day we met. This latest…scoop…from the *Observer* is not only shoddy journalism, it's a bunch of rubbish."

"Of course it is." As Tim set down his cup of coffee, Amy noticed that his hand wasn't quite steady. Sometimes she forgot that his feelings ran as deep as Heather's. He just did a better job masking them under a take-charge, let's-get-down-to-business attitude. "The question is, what do we do?"

"Ignore it," Chris advised. "If we do anything to acknowledge the story, it will just prolong its life."

"Chris is right," Amy agreed.

"What about Dad?" Heather interjected. "Should we tell him?"

"No." Tim's tone was decisive.

"That backfired the last time we tried to

keep something from him. I hated the way he found out about Jeremy's leaving town," Nora reminded them.

"He's in a private room at the hospital, pretty much in isolation," Tim countered. "The staff can be warned to keep quiet about this, and we're already screening visitors. I don't think he needs the added worry." He shot Amy a look, as if daring her to disagree with his next comment. "Despite Strickland's reassurance that stress didn't make Dad more susceptible to this fungal infection, I, for one, see no reason to put that theory to a further test."

Amy surprised him by agreeing. "I don't want to take any chances, either. I vote that we keep this under wraps until we can get to the bottom of it. I think we should do some digging and see if we can put a name on the 'reliable source' that the *Observer* has been quoting in its stories."

"There's nothing we can do from a legal standpoint to force them to reveal their sources," Chris cautioned his family.

"Maybe not, but we can keep our collective ears to the ground, can't we?" Heather planted her hands on her hips, worry and anger vying for prominence on her face.

"Somebody is trying to make our lives miserable, and I'd like to know who."

"Trying?" Tim raised an eyebrow at his sister.

"We have had more placid times," Nora conceded with a sigh. "But I have great faith that if we put our trust in God, He'll see us through this storm. And we'll emerge the stronger for it."

Instead of responding, Tim turned away to reach for his coffee. At least the rest of the siblings gathered in this room today could take some comfort in their faith, Amy reflected. Without that rock to cling to, these past few months would have been difficult to bear. Sometimes she wondered how Tim managed. And she prayed that he wouldn't always have to face troubled times alone, that someday he, too, would find his way to the Lord.

"I'll talk to the staff at the hospital right away about keeping this latest development quiet," Nora continued. "I don't think we'll have any problem. When your father is stronger, I'll share it with him. But I do agree that for right now, he doesn't need that kind of anxiety. It may not hurt his recovery, but I'm sure it wouldn't help, either."

Taking a deep breath, Nora rose. When she spoke, there was a suspicious gleam of moisture in her eyes. "I can't thank you all enough for taking time out of your busy days to come out here this morning. I don't know what I would have done throughout this ordeal if it wasn't for my wonderful children. You've been such a blessing to me."

Heather stepped forward and enfolded her mother in a warm embrace. "There's nowhere else we could be." Her own voice was tearful.

"I know that, dear. And I also know deep in my heart that Jeremy and Melissa are with us in spirit, as well. And I look forward to the day when we're all back together again."

As Amy said her own goodbyes and headed out to her car, she couldn't help but admire her mother's perennial optimism. No matter how bad things got, no matter how many new gauntlets were flung at her feet, she picked them up and just kept going. Sustained by her faith, strengthened by the love of her family, guided by hope, she had never stopped believing in happy endings. Aided in part, no doubt, by the fact that she'd spent the past thirty-five years married to the man of her dreams. A true romance if ever there had been one.

Amy wished she had her mother's fortitude and positive attitude. Although she'd never been a quitter, recent events had conspired to discourage her. And her one romance had gone sour years before when Bryan walked away. Yes, he was back. And yes, last Thursday night after their impromptu pizza dinner she'd glimpsed, for a brief instant, a glimmer of attraction that had made her believe his feelings for her might be deepening. But it had come and gone so fast that she wondered now if it had simply been wishful thinking on her part. Or perhaps he'd just been remembering happier times and succumbed to a moment of nostalgia.

It would be wonderful to recapture the closeness they had once shared. Seeing him again had rekindled all the feelings she'd long ago buried deep in the recesses of her heart. As she'd watched him with his son, learned of his devotion to his wife, grown to admire his sense of duty, she'd realized that the boy she'd once loved had become a man, with a deep maturity honed from hardship and loss and sacrifice. Not only had her love flamed to life again, it had grown and blossomed, like a seedling that sends down deep, anchoring roots to nourish it through adversity.

Now wasn't the time to think about romance, of course. Not with all of the other problems facing the family. But one of these days, if her mother's prediction came true and all of the issues were resolved, maybe then Amy would allow herself to once more believe in happy endings. Just as Nora did.

Chapter Twelve

The breakfast crowd was out in full force, and Bryan hesitated in the doorway as he surveyed the packed dining area at Betty's Bakeshoppe. There didn't seem to be a vacant table in the place. He should have made himself some oatmeal when he fixed Dylan's breakfast, as was his typical routine. Except there hadn't been time. Not after his son suddenly remembered that it was his turn to bring treats for the class, vaulting their usual laid-back start to the day into high gear. Bryan had thrown together a lunch for Dylan, rushed him through breakfast and hustled him out so they could swing by the bakery before heading for school.

At the enticing aromas wafting his way from the kitchen, Bryan's stomach rumbled.

He supposed he could just order takeout, but it would have been nice to sit for a few minutes and get a second wind before jumping into the hectic office routine.

"Amy's over there, if you're looking for an empty seat," Betty offered as she passed by, balancing a loaded tray. She gestured toward a far corner with her free hand.

Taking another look, he spotted her. It was no wonder he'd missed her on his first scan. She was tucked into one of the tiny booths for two in a shadowy corner, her elbow on the table, her head propped in her hand. And from her morose expression, Bryan suspected she wasn't in the mood for company. Had something else happened? he wondered. Not that it was any of his business, of course. But the uncharacteristic droop of her shoulders tugged at his heart, and he knew he couldn't just walk away to let her deal with her latest problem alone. He'd think about why later.

By the time he reached her side, she'd lifted her coffee cup and was staring into the murky depths. She didn't even notice him until he was standing right beside her, and when she looked up her expression went from glum to surprised to curious in a heartbeat.

"Hi." Bryan tried to smile, not sure of his

welcome after their near-kiss the week before. "The place is full, so Betty suggested I claim the empty seat at your table."

After giving the room a quick glance, she inclined her head toward the opposite side of the tiny booth. "Help yourself."

As he slid onto the seat, she reached for the copy of the *Observer* that lay in his place.

"Supporting the competition?" he teased, hoping to elicit a smile.

Instead, the tense line of her face tightened. She was tempted to tell him what she'd like to do to the competition, but a lady didn't use language like that. Nor did a Christian. For a second she hesitated, loath to share the latest sordid installment in the Hamilton family saga with him, but he'd find out soon enough anyway. In silence, she unfolded the paper to the gossip column and pushed it in front of him.

He continued to look into her troubled eyes for a second before shifting his focus to the headline. A shock wave rippled through him as the words sank in, and he scanned the first few lines of the story. A "reliable source" had supplied much of the information for the piece, which was filled with innuendo. Though Wallace Hamilton was never mentioned by name, it was clear that the headline referred to him. No wonder Amy was upset.

When he looked up, Amy spoke before he could say a word. "It's all garbage."

"Well now, I sure hope that's not a comment about the fine food at the Bakeshoppe." Betty's smile, as she withdrew her order pad, communicated just how preposterous such a notion could be. "Bryan, I know you want coffee. Black. What else can I offer you this…"

Her voice trailed off and, despite Amy's distraction, Betty's abrupt pause caught her attention—and Bryan's. They both looked up to find her staring at the headline in the *Observer*, an odd expression on her face. Her smile had faded, and her skin had taken on a gray cast.

"Betty? Are you okay?" Amy half rose and reached out a hand to the owner.

With obvious effort, Betty smiled. At least her lips turned up. But Amy could see no humor in her expression. "Yes. I'm fine. I just remembered something I was supposed to handle first thing this morning. Let me send Wendy out to take your order."

Before Amy or Bryan could question her further, Betty turned on her heel and hurried toward the kitchen.

"What's with her?" Bryan stared after her, puzzled.

"I have no idea." Amy looked back down at the paper. "Maybe she just felt awkward. She's been a friend of the family for years, and there's no comfortable way to discuss a situation like this."

Once more, Bryan examined the story. "Any idea who the 'reliable source' is?"

"No."

"What are you going to do about it?"

"Nothing. We all met with Mom this morning. We agreed that responding in any way would just give the story a higher profile. We're going to ignore it…and keep our ears to the ground in the hopes that we can figure out who's supplying the *Observer* with this supposedly reliable information."

"Sounds like a good plan."

Just then Wendy, Betty's youngest daughter, came up beside their table. Amy turned to her in concern. "Is your mom all right?"

"Yes. She's just been feeling a little under the weather lately. What can I get for you today?"

As Wendy spoke, she looked everywhere but at Amy. Also odd. But Amy was up to her ears in odd things right now. She couldn't handle even one more.

After they gave their order, Bryan turned his full attention to Amy. Unlike Wendy, he had no problem looking directly at her. And considering the probing, appraising look in his eyes, Amy suddenly decided she preferred Wendy's evasive maneuvers.

"I'm sorry about this." He tapped the paper with his finger.

"Thanks. Just when I think things can't get any worse, wham…something else comes along to knock us down."

"Your family has had its share of bad breaks in the past few months, that's for sure."

"Enough to last a lifetime."

"How's your mom holding up?"

"She's a rock. She has this amazing optimism, and she keeps insisting that everything will turn out fine. We're all trying to follow her example and stay positive."

"Her oldest daughter seems to be doing a good job of that."

Although his comment warmed her, Amy knew better. "I wish that was true. I try to keep an upbeat attitude in public, but at home, when I'm alone…it's hard to maintain."

"You seemed okay Thursday night." His voice took on a deeper, more intimate tone.

"I wasn't alone Thursday night."

An ember flared to life in his eyes for a brief instant, but long enough to send a surge of warmth to her cheeks. "I had a good time."

"So did I." Her voice came out as a mere whisper.

He looked down at her hands, which were gripped around her coffee mug. For a second, she thought he was going to reach over and enfold them in his strong, capable fingers. Wanted him to, in fact. As she held her breath, the boisterous sounds of the Bakeshoppe receded, and the frantic beat of her own heart filled her ears. She loosened her hold on the mug, waiting, watching. Bryan's eyes had a cautious, testing-the-waters kind of look, and she sensed that something had changed in their relationship since Thursday. That maybe, just maybe, he was beginning to open himself up to the possibility of a new romance—with her. And all at once, despite all the problems that had beset the Hamilton family, she thought about happy endings…and began to believe— as she had once, long ago—that perhaps there might be one in her future after all.

"Excuse me."

With a start, Amy looked up at Wendy, who stood beside the table juggling two plates. From her tone, Amy realized that she must have repeated that phrase at least a couple of times. As Amy withdrew her hands and Wendy set a bagel and cream cheese in front of her, she saw Heather wave at her from across the room, then weave toward her with a purposeful stride.

"I thought you might be here." Her sister drew up beside them and shot Bryan a quick look. "Hi. Sorry to interrupt." Then she turned her attention back to Amy. "The designer just called. There's a problem with the images for that story on the new Asian restaurant in Nashville. He needs to talk to you right away. If he can't get them to the printer today, we could miss our press date."

Taking one final swig of coffee, Amy grabbed her bagel and slid out of the booth. Although she was sorry they'd been interrupted, she knew that a public place like the Bakeshoppe wasn't the best setting in which to move her relationship with Bryan to the next level, if that was even what he had in mind. Not with the *Observer*'s spy hanging around. Discretion had to be the operative word for every member of the Hamilton family right now.

"Sorry to desert you," she told Bryan as she stood. "Duty calls."

"I understand. I'll be over in a few minutes."

"Don't rush. Enjoy your breakfast."

As she walked away, Amy had a feeling that he was following her progress. She told herself not to look back, that she'd only be disappointed if he was focused on his scrambled eggs and bacon instead of her. But when she reached the door, she couldn't resist a quick peek over her shoulder. And she wasn't disappointed.

He was staring after her, a pensive expression on his face, his breakfast untouched in front of him. When he realized she was looking at him, he started, then raised his hand, picked up his fork and began eating.

But the soft, speculative look in his unguarded eyes in the seconds before he shuttered them warmed her heart. And gave wings to her hope.

Wow.

As Amy finished reading Bryan's interview with Dan Marconi, that was the only word that seemed adequate to describe the story. It was a stellar piece of reporting, one destined to garner national attention for *Nashville Living*, given the reclusive nature of the hometown novelist.

But then, everything Bryan had written

since he'd joined the staff had been outstanding. His debut column on family issues was already receiving rave reviews, and several other shorter pieces reflected an exceptional flair. This story, however, was phenomenal. He'd captured the essence of the man in an urbane, articulate, sometimes witty style that took Amy's breath away. He'd always been a very good writer, even back in high school. But in the years since he'd left Davis Landing, he'd become a master at the craft.

"Pretty good, huh?"

At the sound of Heather's voice, Amy looked up at her sister, who stood in the doorway. "That may be a slight understatement."

"I agree. Got a minute?"

"Sure. Have a seat. What's up?" Heather's expression told Amy that her sister hadn't stopped by for a casual chat. But at least it wasn't a family crisis this time. Amy had come to recognize the distinctive, panicked look Heather wore for those situations. This wasn't one of them. Yet something was wrong.

"I'm afraid I have some bad news." Heather dropped into the chair across from Amy's desk. "Bryan's leaving."

Of all the scenarios Amy's active imagination had conjured up when Heather mentioned bad news, that hadn't been one of them. Shocked, she stared at her sister. "What do you mean, leaving?"

"He's leaving. Not right away. In January. He wanted to give us as much notice as possible."

Still stunned, Amy tried to collect her thoughts. "Did he say why?" And why hadn't he told her himself? The second question went unvoiced, however. After all, he'd gone through the proper chain of command. That was appropriate protocol for business associates. And despite what had happened the prior Thursday, maybe that's all he wanted them to be. Her spirits took a nosedive.

"He told me that he's been talking to a syndication company for months about writing a weekly family issues column," Heather continued. "It sounds like they finally reached an agreement. And it's a great deal for Bryan. He can write from home, which was important to him, because he said he doesn't want Dylan to grow up in day care. And the initial distribution on the column will be more than a hundred newspapers nationwide. I'm happy for him, sad for us. His departure will be a loss to *Nashville Living*."

"Yeah."

"At least we'll have him for a couple more months."

"Yeah."

Leaning forward, Heather searched Amy's face. "Are you okay?"

"Yeah." Realizing that she sounded like a stuck record, Amy forced herself to take a deep breath, then reached for a pile of paper. "I've already reviewed this stack of copy. You can take it with you."

When she held it out to Heather, the pronounced quiver in her hand didn't escape her sister's notice. "Look, I'm sure this is a shock. But he's not leaving town, like the last time. You'll still be able to see him."

"Why would I want to do that?"

Shaking her head, Heather took the papers, shuffled them into a pile and tapped them on the desk into a neat stack. "You don't have to pretend with me. I'm your sister. I figured out a long time ago that Bryan still meant more to you than you ever let on." She headed for the door, pausing on the threshold to throw one parting remark over her shoulder. "And just for the record, I think he feels the same way."

She was gone before Amy could respond. And that was probably a good thing, since she had no idea what she would have said.

* * *

"Got a minute?"

It was the same question Amy had been asked earlier in the day, except this time it came from Bryan instead of Heather.

Since her sister had dropped her bombshell four hours before, Amy had been too distracted to do much of anything. Over and over she'd asked herself what it meant, and over and over the same answer kept coming back— I don't know. Was the motive Bryan had given to Heather—that he wanted to be more available for Dylan—legitimate? Or was he leaving because he didn't want to be around her?

She wanted to believe it was the former. And it did make sense. Bryan was a family man through and through. For him, family came first. Always had, always would. Period. Even if that meant he had to adjust other parts of his life in order to best accommodate the people he loved. She respected that. Understood it better now than ever before, given all the problems her own family faced and the strength they had drawn from each other. Yet the timing seemed suspect. Right when he seemed to be softening in his attitude toward her, he was leaving. Or maybe…could he be running away? Even as that possibility occurred to her, she dismissed it. She'd never known Bryan to run away from anything.

After wrestling with those jumbled thoughts and questions for hours, she still had no answers.

Now Bryan stood at her door, perhaps ready to offer them. And suddenly she wasn't sure she wanted to hear them.

The uncertain look that flashed across Amy's face—a look that bordered almost on fear—confirmed Bryan's suspicion that she'd taken his resignation the wrong way. That's why he'd sought her out. Since she hadn't responded to his first question, he took a step inside. "May I?"

Realizing she hadn't answered his initial query, her neck grew warm and she motioned him in. "Of course."

After closing the door behind him, he took the seat Heather had occupied earlier. "I assume Heather told you about my resignation."

"Yes. We'll be very sorry to lose you. You're an exceptional writer." She tried for a professional, impersonal tone. But the words sounded stilted to her ears.

"I'm not leaving because of us, Amy." As usual, he cut right to the chase.

Her heart stopped, then raced on. "It seems

like a wonderful opportunity. I'm happy for you. And this will give you a chance to be at home with Dylan. It's a perfect arrangement." The words came out in a breathless rush. She knew she hadn't addressed his comment, but she didn't know what to say. She waited for him to take the lead.

"It is. Dylan's spent too much of his life already in day care. He deserves a full-time parent at home. This has nothing to do with us."

"Is there an us?" The question slipped out, soft and tentative. She hadn't meant to voice it, and regretted it once she had. "I'm sorry. That's not appropriate. Forget I asked."

A few beats of silence ticked by as he studied her. He seemed to be debating how to respond, and when he did his reply was careful and deliberate. "I'm working through a lot of stuff right now, Amy. And trying to figure out what God's plan is for me—and for us. I'm not there yet, but I'm getting closer. I just need some time to sort things out."

In an instant, Amy was transported back eleven years, to the Christmas of her freshman year in college. To the night she'd told Bryan that she needed time and space. She supposed turnabout was fair play. But for the first time she understood how he must have felt back then. And how difficult it must have been for him to live with the uncertainty of not knowing if the feelings of the woman he loved matched his.

But what choice did she have? As always, Bryan had been honest. He'd recognized that there was something between them, just as she had. Based on their history and his subsequent marriage, it wasn't surprising that he wanted to proceed with caution. All she could do was hope that in time he might realize that, despite their past, they could still build a future together. And in the meantime, it couldn't hurt to give him a glimpse of what was in her heart.

Summoning up her courage, she looked across her desk, into the deep green eyes that had once softened with love and warmed her like sunshine after a spring rain. Someday, if God smiled on her, she'd see that look again. For now, she was happy that at least the acrimony that had been in their depths when he'd first returned had vanished.

"Take whatever time you need, Bryan. I'll wait around."

He seemed surprised by her quiet response, almost as if he'd expected her to shut down emotionally or send him packing. And then the most extraordinary thing happened. He didn't say a word. But for just a moment, one brief instant before he stood and walked out the door, the sun peeked through the clouds in his eyes, sending a ray of warmth that went straight to her heart.

Chapter Thirteen

❧

"Hi, Amy. It's me, Dylan."

Amy's lips curved into a smile and she leaned back in her desk chair. The weather might be raging outside, but the little boy's voice—even if it did sound congested—brightened her day. "Hi, Dylan. Do you have a cold?"

"Uh-huh. I had to stay home from school today. But Dad says I'll feel better tomorrow. Anyway, I tried to call you at home, but I got your machine. So I called the operator, and she found your work number for me. I copied it down all by myself."

The pride in his voice widened Amy's smile. "I'm impressed. That's a lot of numbers to write."

"Yeah. Anyway, I wondered if you could come and eat dinner with us on Sunday."

Taken aback, Amy debated how to respond as a flash of lightning zigzagged across the sky outside her window, followed by an unsettling crash of thunder. "Does your dad know that you're inviting me?"

"Not 'zactly. But at the park last Sunday, he told me that you eat by yourself a lot, and when I asked him if you could come and have dinner with us later at Grandpa's house, he said it wasn't polite to invite people at the last minute. That's why I called tonight. To be polite. Can you come, Amy?"

The hopeful note in his voice tugged at her heart. Of course, Bryan had no idea his son had called. And no doubt he'd be less than thrilled when he found out. He'd been laying low ever since his visit to her office earlier in the week.

As Amy tried to come up with a way to turn Dylan down without hurting his feelings, she heard muffled voices in the background, just like the last time the little boy had called to issue an invitation. Now, as then, Bryan intervened.

"Amy?"

"Hi, Bryan."

"Sorry about this. I had a long talk with Dylan the first time he called with an impromptu invitation. I'll have to try again."

On the last occasion, Amy had more or less

invited herself to James's retirement party. She wasn't about to repeat that mistake. Especially since Bryan had asked for time to sort through his issues. "It's not a problem, Bryan. I enjoy talking to him."

"I think the feeling is mutual."

Another crash of thunder boomed, rattling the windows, and Amy stared into the darkness outside. Rain pelted against the building, sending wide streams of water coursing down the glass. She wasn't looking forward to making her meals-on-wheels rounds tonight. But the sooner she got rolling, the sooner she could get home.

"Don't worry about the call, Bryan. Look, I've got to run. I'm going to try and get a jump on my meal deliveries in case the storm gets worse. Tell Dylan that I appreciate the invitation and that I'll see him at church on Sunday."

Silence greeted her words, and for a second Amy wondered if the lightning had knocked out the phones. "Bryan?"

"Yeah. I'm here." He'd forgotten about Amy's Friday night obligation. As he'd driven home through the raging storm, he'd been focused on Dylan. Although he'd talked to his son in the morning and afternoon, and his father had assured him that the little boy was doing fine, he'd been anxious and on edge all day. His worry about his son had been assuaged when he'd arrived home and seen for himself that the youngster was okay. Now another worry took its place. "Listen, the storm's pretty bad. Can someone else run the route for you tonight?"

Touched by his concern, Amy leaned back in her chair. "No. We're always short-handed as it is. Besides, I've delivered in all kinds of weather. It won't be a problem. In a couple of hours I'll be at home sitting in front of my fireplace."

For a second, an appealing image of Amy curled up in front of a roaring fire—with him by her side—flashed across Bryan's mind. But he squelched it at once. Just a few days before, he was the one who had asked for time. He couldn't very well invite himself over to her place. In any case, the issue was Amy's safety, not a romantic rendezvous, he reminded himself, refocusing his thoughts. If his father hadn't taken off for a movie with a friend, Bryan would have offered to sub for her himself. As it was, his hands were tied. "Could it wait until tomorrow, in the daylight?"

"No. These people count on the meals. I couldn't in good conscience send anyone to bed hungry."

That was a tough argument to refute. Nevertheless, tonight wasn't a good time to be on the road. The lashing rain and fierce wind had spooked even him on his short drive home. Of course, Davis Landing wasn't that large. It wouldn't take Amy that long to complete her deliveries. And if she had any problems, help would be nearby.

"Okay. But…be careful."

"I'll be fine. Tell Dylan I'll see him soon."

As she placed the phone back in its cradle, another flash of lightning sizzled across the valley, illuminating the river below in an eerie light. Though she'd assured Bryan that she'd be okay, in truth she wasn't looking forward to the next couple of hours. The rural roads were dark and sparsely traveled, and in weather like this she could run into flash flooding. But she knew the trouble spots. As long as she was careful and took her time, there shouldn't be any problems.

With a sigh of relief, Amy eased out of the gravel driveway, pulled onto the paved secondary road and pointed her car toward home. All her meals had been delivered, and the gratitude of her clients had more than made up for the kink in her neck—the result of two white-knuckled hours behind the steering wheel. Other than the pain in her neck, though, she was no worse for wear.

As she'd forged on through the gale, however, she'd realized that Bryan's warnings had been justified. The Cumberland River valley was prone to storms this time of year, often remnants of hurricanes hundreds of miles away. The most recent tropical storm had done a number on the Gulf coast and was now giving Tennessee a sample of its waning wrath. The storm had raged all day, and even now the wind was still howling. Tree limbs were down everywhere, but at least none had fallen across the road.

Only when Amy headed into the home stretch toward town did she begin to relax. In less than fifteen minutes, she could put on her warm, fuzzy slippers and curl up in front of her fireplace. A cup of hot chocolate would be just the thing to chase away the chill, she decided. Then she'd check in with her mother to get an update on her father's infection, which was continuing to respond to treatment. At least there'd been good news on that front in recent days. After she relaxed a bit, she might broil a…

An odd sound from her car suddenly

intruded on her pleasant line of thought, and she frowned. At first, she couldn't figure out what the noise was, and she reduced her pressure on the gas pedal, straining to listen. Within seconds, however, she didn't have to strain, or to wonder. The distinctive *thlump, thlump, thlump* could be produced by only one thing: a flat tire.

Easing her car off the road onto the almost nonexistent shoulder, she shut off the engine, rested her hands on top of the wheel and let her forehead drop forward. Talk about bad timing. In another few minutes she would have been home. Still, it could have been worse, she consoled herself. She did have her cell phone, after all. Help was just a call away.

But her peace of mind was short-lived. When she pulled the phone out of her purse and tried to turn it on, she realized with a sinking feeling that the battery was dead. Although her phone had gotten shoved into a corner a couple of times in the past, depressing the on button and draining the battery, it had never before happened at a critical time. As Vera Mae was always fond of saying, however, there was a first time for everything.

Considering the circumstances, Amy knew her options were limited. And walking the re-

maining few miles to town wasn't one of
them. Even though the weather had tapered
off a bit, she wasn't inclined to set out on
another trek in the three-inch heels she still
hadn't gotten rid of. Been there, done that.
And this time there would be no Bryan to
come to her rescue.

She could sit the storm out until someone
missed her, but since tomorrow was
Saturday and she'd had no specific plans,
her absence might not be noticed until
Sunday. Scratch that plan.

Nor would it be logical to wait for another
car to come along. The secondary road wasn't
traveled much even in good weather, and she
doubted whether anyone would be on it
tonight. At least not anyone in their right
mind. A scary thought if ever there was one,
considering her isolated, vulnerable situation.
Well, she just wouldn't go there, she decided,
making a concerted effort to channel her brain
in a different direction.

She mulled over her final option: Change
the tire. She didn't relish tackling that job in
this weather, but at least she knew how to do
it. Chris had insisted several years before that
all the Hamilton women learn a few self-help
techniques for emergencies, including chang-

ing a tire. No one had grumbled more loudly than she about his edict. Now she was glad he'd been adamant. Though she'd never changed a tire by herself, she remembered the instructions and was confident she could handle it. Of course, she'd prefer to be in jeans and a sweatshirt. But she'd cope.

After flipping on her emergency blinkers, she rummaged in her glove compartment for a flashlight, trying to psych herself up for the task at hand. She could do this. Of course she could. After all, she was an independent, capable woman, perfectly able to take care of herself. She didn't need a knight on a white horse to rescue her and solve all her problems. That was for fairy tales, not real life.

But as she stepped out into the cold rain and a shiver ran through her, she couldn't help wishing that just this once, that particular fairy tale would come true.

"Hello. This is Amy. I can't take your call right now. Please leave a message and I'll get back to you as soon as possible."

His mouth thinning in frustration, Bryan replaced the receiver and planted his fists on his hips. Although he'd told himself all evening that Amy would be fine, in the end he'd been worried enough to call her condo, knowing he'd never be able to sleep until he was sure she'd arrived home safely. Except no one had answered. Not the first time he'd tried, nor the second time, nor this time.

She might have stopped somewhere else, but he doubted it. She'd sounded anxious to get home. In fact, she'd said she hoped to be in front of her fireplace in a couple of hours. That had been at five-thirty. It was now eight o'clock.

Bryan forced himself to wait another ten minutes, then tried her number again, with the same result. As his panic began to escalate, he dug through his wallet and withdrew a card containing emergency off-hours numbers for key personnel at *Nashville Living*. Without stopping to second-guess himself, he punched in Heather's home number, his grip on the phone tightening when there was no answer after several rings. Just when he was expecting yet another answering machine to kick in, a breathless voice greeted him.

"Heather?"

"Bryan?" Her voice sounded uncertain.

"Yeah. Look, sorry to bother you at home, but have you heard from Amy tonight?"

"Amy? No. Why?" Now her voice was puzzled.

"I've been trying her condo, and I'm not getting any answer."

"Is there a problem?"

"That's what I'm trying to find out." He raked his fingers through his hair. "I spoke with her just before she left work to do her meals-on-wheels deliveries, and I warned her about the storm. She promised to be careful, but the roads are bad and…" His voice trailed off.

"Yeah. I see what you mean." Now Heather's voice was laced with concern as well. "Especially considering her isolated route."

The knot in Bryan's stomach tightened. "What do you mean?"

"She makes rural deliveries."

Another wave of panic washed over him. If he'd known she had a rural run, he wouldn't have backed off as easily when he was talking to her earlier. "Do you know her route?"

"No. But Dawn does. Tim's secretary. They sub for each other on occasion."

"Do you have her number?"

"Sure. Hang on." A few seconds later, she recited it for him. "What are you going to do?"

"Get the route from Dawn and call the people she was supposed to deliver to. Then I'll try Amy again, and if there's still no answer I'll drive out there."

"Could you or Amy call me later? Just so I know everything's okay?"

"Sure."

Ten minutes later, after a quick call to Dawn, Bryan had a list of Amy's clients and their phone numbers. Calls to each place confirmed that she'd come and gone. Her last stop had been an hour before. After one more futile call to her condo, Bryan bundled up Dylan and headed for the door.

"Where are we going, Dad?" Dylan asked.

He hated to take his son out in this kind of weather, but worry for Amy overrode his concerns for Dylan's improving cold. "We're going to look for Amy. She's out in the country, and I think she might be stuck somewhere." He tried to keep his tone conversational. Experience had taught him that kids were hypersensitive to the nuances of grown-up moods.

Dylan's face brightened. "Can I help?"

"Sure thing. Just keep a sharp lookout while we drive, okay? And let me know if you see anything."

Since Amy had finished all of her deliveries, Bryan headed toward her last call. The rural area around Davis Landing was crisscrossed with a network of small, two-lane roads, and he knew she could have taken a number of routes. But considering the weather, he opted for the one that he thought was the most direct.

That, however, proved a dead end—literally. A creek had overrun its banks and washed across the road, rendering it impassable and dangerous. Bryan knew firsthand about the hazards of flash flooding. A good buddy of his from high school had almost drowned when his car was swept off the road after he'd attempted to cross a flooded creek just like this.

Fighting down his escalating panic, and straining to see through the dark, Bryan scanned the creek bed for any sign that Amy had run into similar trouble. *Lord, please keep her safe!* he prayed.

"Is she here, Dad?" Dylan spoke from the back seat, his voice uncertain and a little scared.

"I don't see her. But I'm going to take a closer look, okay?"

"It's dark here."

"I'm not going far. I promise. I'll leave the headlights on, and you'll be able to see me, okay?"

"Okay, I guess."

Turning up the collar of his jacket, Bryan exited the car and headed toward the creek for a closer look, trying to remain calm. But as he peered into the dark, swirling water, he knew that any attempt to hang on to his composure was destined for failure. And with a sudden jolt, he knew why. He had come to care deeply about Amy. So deeply that it scared him. So deeply that somewhere along the way his feelings had evolved into love.

As Bryan stared at the creek, oblivious to the cold rain seeping through his jacket, he thought back a few days, to when he'd told Amy that he needed time to sort out his feelings. Now he realized that hadn't been true. He knew, as surely as he knew that the sun would rise tomorrow, that the woman he'd once loved, the woman who had matured and grown and changed, had once again stolen his heart. And deep inside, he'd known it for some time. But he'd been afraid. Afraid to take another chance on love. Yes, he'd been concerned about dishonoring the memory of his love for Darlene. But Pastor Abernathy had helped set his mind at ease about that. The thing that was holding him back was fear. After the losses he'd already suffered, he hadn't been willing to take the risk of loving again.

Now, as he stood watching the gentle stream that had been transformed within minutes to a rushing river, he was reminded how fast things can change. And how quickly roads can be blocked and opportunities snatched away—sometimes just because people waited too long, thinking time would reveal the answers that were already in their hearts, just waiting for release. Often it wasn't time that was needed, he realized, but courage.

With sudden resolve, Bryan returned to the car, backed into a turn and set off again. He'd find Amy. And when he did, he wasn't going to make her wait another minute for an answer to her question about whether there was an "us."

They drove in silence for a few minutes, until Dylan's excited voice called out, "Look, Dad! There's a car!"

He'd seen it at the same time, in between swipes of the wiper blades, and he'd immediately recognized the dark blue sedan as Amy's Toyota. It was on the opposite side of the road, half on the shoulder. Pulling over to the side, he jammed on the brake and opened his door, speaking to Dylan as he slid out of his seat. "I'll be right back. Sit tight, okay?"

Without waiting for a response, he strode toward Amy's car. When he realized it was empty, his gut tightened as a dozen possible scenarios flashed through his mind, none of them pretty. Then he noticed an odd glow coming from the shoulder side of the car. Proceeding with caution, he rounded the vehicle, and almost collapsed with relief. Amy wasn't hurt. Or worse. She was changing a tire. Or trying to, he amended. She'd propped a flashlight on the ground, angling it toward the tire, and was cranking the car up with a jack a fraction of an inch at a time. So focused was she on her task that she was oblivious to his presence. Although her blond hair had been darkened by the rain, there was grease on her cheek, and her clothes were soaked, she'd never looked more beautiful to him.

When he stepped forward, Amy turned. With the flashlight shining in her face, blinding her, all she saw was a looming presence in the blackness. Her eyes widened, and with a startled gasp she groped for the lug wrench and attempted to stand. Instead, she lost her balance and sat back, hard.

Bryan went down at once on one knee beside her, letting the light illuminate his face. "It's me, Amy. I'm sorry I startled you." With a gentle hand, he pushed some of the wet hair back from her pale face.

"Bryan?" Her voice was so shaky even she didn't recognize it. "Wh-what are you doing here?"

"Looking for you." He pried the wrench out of her fingers, then stood, pulling her up beside him in one smooth motion. She was shaking badly, and he wrapped his arms around her, holding her close, stroking her back as he thanked God for keeping her safe during the storm. "I was so worried," he murmured, his voice close to her ear, his breath warm on her face.

As Amy stood there in the rain, within the protective circle of Bryan's strong arms, she could feel the pounding of his heart and knew that this moment was the one she had been wishing for for more years than she cared to count. Until the past few days, she hadn't let herself believe that it might ever arrive. But now, in her heart, she sensed that it had, that her time of waiting was past. Her knight had come riding by after all, bringing with him the hope of a happy ending.

Bryan held her for a long time, though not long enough. Then again, even forever wouldn't be long enough, Amy thought, sorry when he at last pulled back. But she was only sorry for an instant, because as he stared down at her, warmth flooded his eyes, chasing away the chill in the autumn air. It was the same warmth she remembered from long ago. The warmth that spelled *love* in capital letters. The warmth she had seen in his eyes that rainy day years before, when he'd kissed her for the first time in Sugar Tree Park.

As she looked back at him, her own eyes alight with love, his darkened with an intensity that took her breath away. Then he leaned down to claim her lips in a gentle kiss of reunion, of healing and hope. Time stopped, and she lost herself in the wonder of his embrace.

"Hey, Dad, you're all wet."

When Dylan's voice at last intruded on her consciousness, breaking the romantic spell, she made a halfhearted effort to pull back. But Bryan's lips lingered on hers, as if he couldn't bear to release them. When he at last broke contact, the look on his face left Amy breathless and told her that he considered this only a brief interruption.

Together, they turned toward Bryan's car. Dylan had unhooked his seat belt and rolled down the window, and his arms were resting on the windowsill, propping up his chin. A grin split his face from ear to ear.

With a chuckle, Bryan tucked Amy closer to his side. "You're right, champ. But the rain has stopped. And you know what? Tomorrow is going to be a sunny day."

Then he looked down at Amy once more, his eyes warm with love and filled with promise. And she didn't have to wait until tomorrow to see the sun. It was already shining in her heart.

* * * * *

Dear Reader,

As I write this letter, summer is waning. After a long dry spell, the parched ground is yearning for autumn's promise of cooler days and refreshing rains, which will strengthen and renew the plants that have begun to wither.

Often, our lives mirror the seasons of nature. Sometimes we go through dry spells when we yearn for emotional or spiritual refreshment. In *The Family Man,* both Bryan and Amy experience such a time. But with trust in God, and blessed by His renewing grace, they find the courage to take a second chance on love.

The Family Man marks the first time I have participated in a continuity series, in which each book is written by a different author. Although every book is a complete romance in itself, each also carries certain plot elements forward until all the loose ends are tied up in the final book. It has been an interesting experience, and I hope you enjoy all six Davis Landing novels.

Please watch for my next Love Inspired book, *Rainbow's End,* coming in January. And be sure to check my Web site at www.irenehannon.com for the latest news on my upcoming releases.

In the meantime, have a wonderful autumn and a blessed holiday season!

Irene Hannon

QUESTIONS FOR DISCUSSION

1. As the eldest, high-achiever daughter, Amy has always been a role model for her sisters. But her success and confidence have also been somewhat intimidating, sometimes giving both sisters a feeling of inferiority. As she matured and found her way back to her faith, Amy realized this and now makes an effort to bolster their self-esteem. What are some examples of this from *The Family Man?* What role might her renewed faith have played in her heightened sensitivity?

2. Despite their different personalities, the Hamilton siblings are all quite close. How have they created such a strong family bond? Why are family ties important? What are the hallmarks of a strong family?

3. Although Amy was eminently qualified to take over the helm of Hamilton Media when Jeremy left, her brother was chosen instead. How did she come to terms with this? Have you ever been passed over for something you felt you deserved? How did you deal with the jealousy and resentment you might have experienced? How did your faith help you through this difficult time?

4. When Bryan returns to Davis Landing, it takes him quite awhile to realize—and admit—that Amy has changed. Why was that hard for him? Why did he fight the attraction? Have you ever had a preconceived image of a person? How did that affect your relationship with them, especially in the beginning?

5. Why did Amy and Bryan break up when they were in college? If the timing of their first meeting had been different, might their relationship have progressed differently? How? How important is timing in romance?

6. When *The Family Man* starts, Amy's once-lax faith has stabilized and strengthened, while Bryan's once-solid faith has become shaky. Why? How does Bryan find his way back to the Lord? What events in your life have affected your faith journey? How?

7. Nora chose not to tell Wallace about Jeremy's departure. Though her motive was well-intentioned, her husband found out anyway. Should she have kept this secret? What were the consequences? Have you ever kept information to yourself that you could have shared? Why? Was it a good decision? Why or why not? What factors should be considered in making a decision of this kind?

Tim Hamilton finds he's met his match in
THE HAMILTON HEIR,
by Valerie Hansen,
coming in October 2006,
only from Steeple Hill Love Inspired.

Please turn the page for a sneak peek.

Five p.m. arrived before Dawn knew it. Normally, she looked forward to taking the meals to her regular meals-on-wheel's customers. This evening, however, she was decidedly uneasy. Not only was she faced with having Tim Hamilton acting as her chauffeur, she'd realized belatedly that he was going to have to drive her home, too. Hamilton Media was located in Davis Landing, in the high-rent district along the Cumberland River, while she lived in Hickory Mills, a place often referred to as the "wrong side of the tracks." She didn't relish having her hyper-critical boss see her modest apartment, even from the outside.

She considered phoning for a taxi, then changed her mind for fear of offending him. The door to Tim's office stood ajar and she could hear him talking on the phone, so she waited till he'd ended his conversation before rapping on the door and easing it open a bit farther.

"Mr. Hamilton?"

"Yes?"

He had removed his jacket, loosened his pale blue silk tie and rolled up his shirtsleeves, yet his wavy hair was perfectly combed and he looked like a glossy ad for tailored suits or expensive Italian loafers.

Dawn hesitated, then plunged ahead. "All that correspondence you wanted is stacked on my desk, waiting for your signature."

"Good. Thanks."

"I—uh—I thought I'd go home now."

"Is it that late already?"

"I'm afraid so."

"Then we'd better get going." He stood. "Where do you live?"

"Hickory Mills. On Third Street."

"Then let's go. Can't keep hungry folks waiting for their dinner."

"I still feel bad about this. I wouldn't agree to it except—"

"Except I murdered your car. Have you heard anything about its repair or am I going to have to pay for a funeral, instead?"

"Repair. Definitely repairs," Dawn said,

smiling. "The garage called. They promised a price break and I told them to go ahead. I hope that was okay."

"Fine. Very efficient, as usual." He slung his jacket over one shoulder, then joined her at the door. "I was going to do a bit more work before I called it a day, but I guess I can come in early tomorrow. Let's go."

Having to take two steps for each of his long strides, she was nearly running by the time they got to the elevator. He reached out and held the door open for her to pass.

"Thanks," she said. "I'm glad you're not in a hurry. I'd probably have to wear track shoes to keep up with you if you were."

"You were moving pretty fast this morning," Tim countered. "I had to run down the stairs to catch you."

"Good thing you have such long legs then, huh?" Dawn saw him eye her much shorter stature and discerned a touch of wry humor in his expression. "My legs are not too short," she insisted. "They reach all the way to the ground, don't they?"

Tim chuckled. "That they do."

Suddenly, Dawn wished she'd kept her mouth shut instead of calling attention to herself. She wasn't ashamed of her lithe figure or the feminine clothing she favored, she just hadn't meant for her otherwise reserved boss to take special notice. There had been times, ever since she'd started working for him, that she'd secretly wished he'd at least acknowledge her as a living, breathing human being. Now that he had, however, she wasn't so sure she liked it, especially since they were cooped up in a cramped elevator. Alone.

Don't be silly, her sensible side argued. *There's nothing wrong with taking an innocent elevator ride with a man, no matter how handsome and dashing he happens to be.* And there was certainly nothing wrong with Tim Hamilton's manners. He was every bit the perfect Southern gentleman he'd always been.

Particularly in regard to other women, she added contritely. Until today, his suave graciousness had seemed reserved for women he saw socially. Now that Dawn was the recipient of the Hamilton charm, she wasn't sure how she ought to react. One thing was certain, however—this was going to be a very *long* evening.

If she could have been positive the whole unfolding sequence of events was God's idea, maybe meant to show Tim how to appreciate the simple things in life more, she'd have been happier with the situation. Then again, who was she to question her Heavenly Father?

The same silly person I've always been, she answered honestly. Some things were just beyond human comprehension and the only times she got herself into real trouble were when she tried to second-guess the Lord and help Him out.

That ridiculous thought made her smile. As if God wasn't capable to doing anything He wanted whether she cooperated or not!